MW00974982

MULTICULTURAL BIOGRAPHIES COLLECTION

LATINO
BIOGRAPHIES

GLOBE FEARON
EDUCATIONAL PUBLISHER

PARAMUS, NEW JERSEY

Paramount Publishing

Senior Editor: Barbara Levadi
Project Editor: Lynn W. Kloss
Editorial Assistant: Roger Weisman
Writers: Sandra Widener, Nancy Ellis
Production Manager: Penny Gibson
Art Director: Nancy Sharkey
Production Editor: Nicole Cypher
Marketing Manager: Sandra Hutchison
Interior Electronic Design: Joan Jacobus
Photo Research: Jenifer Hixson
Electronic Page Production: Eric Dawson
Cover and Interior Design: B B & K Design, Inc.
Cover Illustration: Jane Sterrett

Copyright © 1995 by Globe Fearon Educational Publisher, a division of Paramount Publishing, 240 Frisch Court, Paramus, New Jersey 07652. All rights reserved. No part of this book may be reproduced or transmitted in any form or by any means, electrical or mechanical, including photocopying, recording, or by any information storage and retrieval system without permission in writing from the publisher.

Printed in the United States of America.   2 3 4 5 6 7 8 9 10 99 98 97 96 95

ISBN: 0-835-90849-6

GLOBE FEARON
EDUCATIONAL PUBLISHER
PARAMUS, NEW JERSEY

Paramount

Paramount Publishing

CONTENTS

You have probably read many biographies during your years in school. Because no biography can describe everything about a person, a biographer usually writes with a focus, or a theme of the subject's life, in mind. A collection of biographies also has a focus, so that if you wanted to learn, for example, about famous scientists or sports figures, you could quickly locate a book that portrays people in these fields.

The biographies presented in this book introduce you to 21 people whose cultural backgrounds are Latino. The book explores their heritages and how these heritages influenced their lives. It also describes how these people became successful in their careers.

The book is divided into four units. Each unit features the life stories of several people whose careers are related to subjects that you study in school. The map of North, Central, and South America on page 1 shows you the locations of places mentioned in the biographies.

In addition, a directory of Career Resources and a Bibliography are located in the back of the book. These resources suggest books, magazines, and agencies that can tell you more about the people and careers discussed.

As you read these biographies, think about the different cultural heritages that are part of the description *Latino*. Notice, also, that even though people around the world have different traditions, all cultures have similarities. By recognizing our similarities and respecting our differences, we can come to know and to understand each other.

ACKNOWLEDGMENTS

p. 4: (top) Phil Cantor, (bottom) Ruben Guzman; **p. 5:** (top) Courtesy of Luis Santeiro, (middle) © Bill Eichner, (bottom) Courtesy of Arte Público Press; **p. 6:** © Phil Cantor; **p. 7:** © Phil Cantor; **p. 16:** © Ruben Guzman; **p. 17:** © Ruben Guzman; **p. 25:** © Jill Wachter; **p. 26:** Courtesy of Luis Santeiro; **p. 34:** © Sara Eichner; **p. 35:** © Bill Eichner; **p. 43:** Courtesy of Arte Público Press; **p. 44:** Courtesy of Arte Público Press; **p. 60:** (top) Social and Public Art Resource Center, (bottom) Reuters/Bettmann; **p. 61:** (top) Wide World, (middle) Courtesy of the Boston Ballet, (bottom) Courtesy of The Puerto Rican Traveling Theatre; **p. 62:** Los Angeles Times Photo; **p. 63:** Social and Public Art Resource Center; **p. 71:** Wide World Photos; **p. 72:** Reuters/Bettmann; **p. 81:** Courtesy of F.A.S.E.; **p. 82:** Wide World Photos; **p. 91:** Wide World Photos; **p. 92:** Courtesy of the Boston Ballet; **p. 99:** Courtesy of The Puerto Rican Traveling Theatre; **p. 100:** Courtesy of The Puerto Rican Traveling Theatre; **p. 116:** (top) Courtesy of F.A.S.E., (bottom) Rick Vargas, The Smithsonian Institute; **p. 117:** (top) Reuters/Bettmann, (middle) © Clara Griffin, (bottom) Courtesy of Adriana Ocampo; **p. 118:** Courtesy of F.A.S.E.; **p. 119:** Courtesy of F.A.S.E.; **p. 127:** The Smithsonian Institute; **p. 128:** Rick Vargas, The Smithsonian Institute; **p. 136:** UPI/Bettmann; **p. 137:** Reuters/Bettmann; **p. 145:** © Patricia Barry Levy; **p. 146:** © Clara Griffin; **p. 154:** Courtesy Adriana Ocampo; **p. 155:** Courtesy Adriana Ocampo; **p. 170:** (top) Wide World Photos, (bottom) Courtesy of Ileana Ros-Lehtinen; **p. 171:** (top right) Courtesy of the Alvarado Construction Company, (top left) Reuters/Bettmann, (bottom right) Reuters/Bettmann, (bottom left) Courtesy of MALDEF; **p. 172:** Wide World Photos; **p. 173:** Wide World Photos; **p. 181:** Courtesy of Ileana Ros-Lehtinen; **p. 182:** Courtesy of Ileana Ros-Lehtinen; **p. 190:** Courtesy of the Alvarado Construction Company; **p. 191:** Courtesy of The Alvarado Construction Company; **p. 199:** Reuters/Bettmann; **p. 200:** Reuters/Bettmann; **p. 208:** Reuters/Bettmann; **p. 209:** Reuters/Bettmann; **p. 217:** Courtesy of MALDEF; **p. 218:** Courtesy of MALDEF.

This map shows the countries and cities in North, Central, and South America
mentioned in this book.

INTRODUCTION

A biography is a portrait of a person presented in words rather than pictures. Details of historical events, personal tragedies and successes, family traits and cultural traditions, and individual talents are often included to help the reader "get to know" the subject.

A biography cannot tell everything about a person. To do this, a biographer would have to write either an enormous book with a great deal of detail about unimportant events or a book that covers each event, even important ones, very quickly. Biographers, then, must choose the areas they wish to explore with care, so that they will help the reader understand at least a part of a person's life fully.

This book introduces you to 21 Latinos. Their biographies focus on three areas: childhood experiences, cultural heritage, and career goals. Although each is Latino, each life story is unique. As you read, you will notice similarities. You will also find that each has his or her own definition of success and of what it means to be Latino.

Childhood experiences often influence the type of individual a person becomes. Particularly exciting or unhappy times can have a major impact. For example, from the time of her birth, Antonia Novello suffered from a painful medical condition. Through several difficult surgical operations, Novello kept sight of her goal: to someday be a doctor so that she might heal others.

Some of the people you will read about do not discuss much about their childhood experiences. For them, achievements later in life are more important.

Cultural heritage includes language, religion, and family structure. Culture is expressed through customs, food and clothing, and behavior, as well as through art, music, and writing. Some Latinos you will read about have been shaped by their heritage. For example, Judith Baca decided early in her career that her art would speak directly to the people in her community.

For others, culture did not become important until adulthood. Luis Santeiro found a sense of his cultural identity as a scriptwriter when he portrayed the difficulties of adjusting to life in a new country: the United States.

Career goals reveal a great deal about a person. You will read how education and hard work were valued by the families described in this book. Some biographies tell of early commitments to career goals. NASA scientist Adriana Ocampo and actor Miriam Colón followed their childhood dreams.

Other Latinos described here changed careers as they matured. Edward James Olmos, for example, wanted to play baseball, switched to music, and finally found acting.

Personal challenges have affected many of the people you will read about. Some have met with prejudice. They have had to decide whether to try to blend in with U.S. culture or to hold onto their own languages and identities.

Several people came to the United States because of unrest in their homelands. Congresswoman Ileana Ros-Lehtinen from Cuba and author Julia Alvarez from the Dominican Republic are two examples. Success in a new country meant having to learn a new language and customs, finding a job, and replacing possessions left behind. Jaime Escalante spent seven years retraining in the United States even though he had been one of Bolivia's best-known teachers.

Others, such as Cabinet member Federico Peña, ballet dancer Fernando Bujones, and corporate executive Roberto Goizueta, grew up under comfortable conditions. Some of their struggles, then, have been internal, questioning how best to combine their Latino and U.S. traditions.

Biographies tell a person's life story, but they can also help the reader discover more about himself or herself. As you read, think about these questions: What do you admire about these people? Which people and careers do you want to learn more about? In short, what do your reactions to these biographies tell you about yourself?

LATINOS IN LITERATURE

In this unit, you will read about five Latino writers. Each has a unique background, yet all have been successful in blending their culture with their craft. As you meet these writers and learn of their diverse heritages, think about how each one has discovered a sense of purpose. How has each author developed a personal style of writing?

Puerto Rican author and artist **Nicholasa Mohr** (nihk-uh-LAH-sah MAWR) knew about the power of imagination from an early age: "I discovered that by making pictures and writing letters I could create my own world . . . like magic."

Growing up in a poor Chicago neighborhood helped Mexican American author **Sandra Cisneros** (sees-NER-ohs) write with a distinct voice: "With words I have the power to make people . . . cry, to make them laugh. It's a powerful thing to make people listen to you."

As a child in Cuba, **Luis Santeiro** (sahn-TAY-roh) loved plays: "I longed to be connected in some way with the making of all that magic." His award-winning scripts deliver this magic to *Sesame Street* audiences.

Although her home in Middlebury, Vermont, is far from the Dominican Republic, author **Julia Alvarez** (AHL-vah-res) thinks often of her former homeland. Her writing depicts the jolt of leaving: "I had to struggle to find words."

The poems of **Tato Laviera** (TAH-toh lah-vee-ER-ah) speak of the Puerto Rican experience in New York City. This best-selling poet and playwright remembers: "There was always a sense of community . . . we had a lot of extended family."

As you read this unit, think about how each writer's experiences influenced his or her choice of subjects. Consider also how writing has shaped the way each person sees the world.

NICHOLASA MOHR

When she was a child, Nicholasa Mohr could not find herself in the books she read. She now draws on her Puerto Rican heritage to create characters for another generation of readers.

It was time for Nicholasa Mohr (nihk-uh-LAH-sah MAWR) to choose a high school. "You won't be going to college," her guidance counselor told her. "Let's find you a nice high school where you can learn to sew."

Mohr felt humiliated[1] and helpless. There was no one to fight for her rights or come to her defense. Her protests were ignored. Mohr recalls, "I felt I had no power and I was being told by someone with power that this is the way it's going to be." Instead, she finally was allowed to attend a high school of fashion and design where she could follow her first love, drawing. Mohr never forgot the counselor's image of her. When she became a writer she used events like this, repeated again and again in her early life, to make her writing more powerful.

Nicholasa Mohr's family immigrated to this country during the Great Depression in the 1930s. They settled in the oldest Spanish-speaking community in New York City, called Spanish Harlem. (See **Did You Know?** on page 11 for more information about Puerto Rican immigration to New York City.) Nicholasa Mohr was born in New York in 1938, the youngest child and only girl of seven children.

When Mohr started elementary school, the family moved to the Bronx, another area of New York City. When she was young, Puerto Rican girls were expected to get married and have children, not work outside the home. "I couldn't imagine myself in that role," she says. "I wanted more for myself." As she grew up with her six older brothers, "Our family still held old-fashioned Puerto Rican concepts about the male and female roles. It was often a struggle for me," she says.

The family struggled in other ways. Mohr's father died when she was eight, and the family lived in poverty. In addition, her mother was often sick. Mohr escaped into her love of art. "From

---

1. **humiliated** (hyoo-MIHL-ee-ayt-uhd) *v.* ashamed; embarrassed

the moment my mother handed me some scrap paper, a pencil, and a few crayons, I discovered that by making pictures and writing letters, I could create my own world . . . like magic. In the small, crowded apartment with my large family, making magic permitted me all the space, freedom, and adventure that my imagination could handle."

Mohr remembers her mother as the one who had faith in her. "My mother would encourage all of us to study and make something of ourselves. Often, she'd look at my drawings and say, '*Mi hijita* (mee ee-HEE-teh) [my little daughter], you are special with these God-given talents. Someday you must study so that you can become an important artist . . . make an important contribution to the world and really be somebody.' These words of encouragement always made me feel better."

Before Mohr began high school, her beloved mother died. Her death was hard on Nicholasa. "My mother's strength and independence served as a strong role model for me," she says. Mohr's aunt, a woman who was often distant and uninvolved, became her guardian.[2]

Mohr learned to be strong. She is also convinced that her artistic talent helped protect her from some of the bigotry other Puerto Rican children in her neighborhood faced. "I used my imagination and was able to create something interesting and pleasing where previously there had been a sense of despair." After finishing a painting or drawing, Mohr says, she could look at a beautiful product of her imagination, and "life would be a little better than before."

After high school, Mohr followed her dream of studying at the Art Students' League in New York. To support herself, she worked as a waitress, an office worker, and a translator. During this time, she saved money to travel to Europe and study art. When it came time to go, however, she realized that she really wanted to study the great painters and muralists of Mexico, who

---

2. **guardian** (GAHR-dee-uhn) *n.* one who takes care of another person

used strong colors and bold designs to express their sense of their culture. "In a profound[3] way, their work spoke to me and my experiences as a Puerto Rican woman born in New York," she says.

When she returned from Mexico, she continued studying, this time at the New School for Social Research in New York City. There she met the man who would become her husband, Irwin Mohr. He was studying for his doctorate in clinical psychology. The couple married in 1958, and had two sons, David and Jason.

In 1970, the family moved to Teaneck, New Jersey. Mohr set up an art studio in the attic of their house. She began to be noticed for her work, which Mohr describes as "filled with bold figures, faces, and various symbols of the city . . . numbers, letters, words, and phrases . . . a kind of graffiti." What Mohr did was turn the graffiti and culture of the streets she knew in New York City into art.

She began to sell her art and to work as an art teacher. Mohr had never thought of writing. Then a publisher asked her to write about her experiences growing up Puerto Rican in New York City. At first, Mohr said no. Then she began thinking about the idea. "I was well aware that there were no books published about Puerto Rican girls, or boys either for that matter. I was also reminded that when I was growing up, I'd enjoyed reading about the adventures of many boys and girls, but I had never really seen myself, my brothers, and my family in those books. We were just not there. I, as a Puerto Rican child, did not exist then . . . and I, as a Puerto Rican woman, did not exist now [in literature]. Finally, I agreed to write fifty pages of short stories, doing the best I could."

Mohr wrote a series of vignettes[4] about growing up as a Puerto Rican girl in New York City. The publisher turned it down. "I think what she expected was something much more sensational," Mohr says. "I had never stolen anything, taken hard

3. **profound** (pruh-FOWND) *adj.* deep; important
4. **vignettes** (vihn-YEHTS) *n. pl.* brief stories or descriptions

drugs, been raped or mugged. So I guess she thought my life was uneventful." Soon another publisher asked Mohr to create a cover for another book. Instead, Mohr brought in her writing.

"Three weeks later, I was astonished when I received a letter offering me a contract and an advance[5] to write a novel based on my short stories." The result was *Nilda,* a story of a young Puerto Rican girl growing up in the Bronx during World War II. In the novel, Mohr describes what it is like to be called "you people" by policemen and even worse names by classmates. In moving detail, she tells the story of a poor girl who is made fun of at camp because she has no real suitcase. The pain comes right out of Mohr's early years. Like Mohr, Nilda uses her imagination to escape the sad reality around her.

The book was an instant success. One critic wrote that *Nilda* was "a significant book, a touchstone[6] by which others may be judged." For the book, Mohr won the Outstanding Book Award in Juvenile Fiction from *The New York Times* in 1973. She also won an award from the Jane Addams Peace Association for *Nilda.* The Society of Illustrators gave Mohr an award for the book's jacket, which she had designed. After *Nilda,* Mohr had a career as a writer as well as an artist.

Other books followed, each a success. Mohr has published *El Bronx Remembered, Felita, In Nueva York,* and a sequel[7] to *Felita,* called *Going Home.* Each book has been greeted as warmly as *Nilda. Felita,* like *Nilda,* expresses some of Mohr's experiences and feelings as a Puerto Rican girl. In *Felita,* a Puerto Rican family decides to move to a better part of town. When they arrive, Felita is treated cruelly by the neighborhood children because of her cultural background. Finally, feeling defeated by the harassment they receive, the family moves back to the old neighborhood. In *Going Home,* Felita and her family spend a

---

5. **advance** (uhd-VANTS) *n.* money paid before work is done
6. **touchstone** (TUCH-stohn) *n.* the standard by which others are judged
7. **sequel** (SEE-kwuhl) *n.* a work that continues the story told in an earlier book, movie, or other story

summer in Puerto Rico. "Felita is a vivid, memorable character, well realized and well developed," wrote a reviewer for the *School Library Journal*. "It is a pleasure to welcome her back."

In 1978, Mohr's husband died. Three years later, her brother died. Mohr kept writing articles, short stories, and books. Her memoir of growing up, *In My Own Words: Growing Up Inside the Sanctuary*[8] *of My Imagination,* was published in 1994.

Although as a young girl, Mohr was not given much encouragement to use her talents, those talents have finally been recognized. Besides the awards for *Nilda,* Mohr won the American Book Award in 1981. In 1986, she was a finalist for the National Book Award. She was awarded an honorary doctorate from the State University of New York in Albany in 1989, and from 1988 to 1990, Mohr was a distinguished visiting professor at Queens College in New York City. Her books have been translated into Spanish and Japanese.

Even though she continues to love art, Mohr has come to believe that in writing she can "draw pictures with words." She says, "Storytelling allows me the freedom to express what I feel most deeply about with greater detail. There is a crying need for what I had to say as a Puerto Rican, as someone living here, and as a woman." As a child, Mohr may have found no books that mirrored her experience, but as an adult, she has made sure that these books exist for those who come after her.

> ***Did You Know?*** *Difficulty finding jobs in Puerto Rico and the hope of better jobs on the mainland has led to the continuing Puerto Rican migration to the United States. The largest number of people arrived between 1945 and the mid-1960s. Because Puerto Rico is a commonwealth of the United States, Puerto Ricans can travel easily between Puerto Rico and the mainland. New York became established as the main destination of migrating Puerto Ricans before World War II. Then, most travel was by boat, and New York was the largest*

---

8. **sanctuary** (SANGK-chuh-wehr-ee) *n.* a place of protection; a haven

port in the United States. After the first immigrants were settled in New York, their relatives and friends came to join them, enlarging the existing Puerto Rican community.

AFTER YOU READ

EXPLORING YOUR RESPONSES

1. Imagine you were Nicholasa Mohr and your guidance counselor told you that you wouldn't be going to college. What might you have done?

2. When she was young, Mohr escaped into her love of art. What other activities can help people turn a bad situation into a good one?

3. Mohr began writing because she did not see herself in the books she read. If you were going to be a writer of books or movies, what might you write about?

4. Mohr's mother encouraged her when she was young. Describe a person who has encouraged you in your life.

5. Mohr has tried to create characters that young people can identify with. Describe a character from a book or movie that you identify with.

UNDERSTANDING WORDS IN CONTEXT

Read the following sentences from the biography. Think about what each underlined word means. In your notebook, write what each word means as it is used in the sentence.

1. Before Mohr began high school, her beloved mother died. . . . Mohr's aunt, a woman who was often distant and uninvolved, became her guardian.

2. Mohr wrote a series of vignettes about growing up as a Puerto Rican girl in New York City.

3. One critic wrote that *Nilda* was "a significant book, a touchstone by which others may be judged."

4. Mohr has published *El Bronx Remembered, Felita, In Nueva York,* and a sequel to *Felita,* called *Going Home.*

5. Her memoir of growing up, *In My Own Words: Growing Up Inside the Sanctuary of My Imagination,* was published in 1994.

RECALLING DETAILS

1. How was Mohr's childhood a struggle?

2. How did Mohr escape unhappiness as a child?

3. Why did Mohr decide to study art in Mexico rather than in Europe?

4. Why did Mohr decide to write about her experiences?

5. How does Mohr think writing is like painting?

UNDERSTANDING INFERENCES

In your notebook, write two or three sentences from the biography that support the following inferences.

1. By becoming an artist and a writer, Mohr was not doing what a Puerto Rican girl was expected to do.

2. Mohr's mother did not follow the traditional views of what Puerto Rican women could do.

3. Mohr was determined to become an artist.

4. Much of what Mohr writes about is inspired by her childhood.

5. Mohr wishes that there had been books like hers when she was growing up.

INTERPRETING WHAT YOU HAVE READ

1. Who was the most important person in Mohr's early life? Why was this person important?

2. Why was imagination so important to Mohr as a child?

3. Why might Mohr prefer Mexican muralists to European artists?

4. What characteristics do you think enabled Mohr to become a successful artist?

5. Why would a critic call *Nilda* "a touchstone by which others may be judged"?

ANALYZING QUOTATIONS

Read the following quotation from the biography and answer the questions below.

> *"Storytelling allows me the freedom to express what I feel most deeply about with greater detail. There is a crying need for what I had to say as a Puerto Rican, as someone living here, and as a woman."*

1. Why does Mohr believe that there is a "crying need" for her writing?

2. What do you think Mohr can do with writing that she cannot do with art?

3. Mohr feels that writing is the best way for her to express her ideas. How might you express your ideas? Explain.

THINKING CRITICALLY

1. What do you think Mohr might have done if she hadn't had a talent for art?

2. Do you agree that Mohr's childhood of bigotry and poverty was important in her becoming an artist? Explain your answer.

3. What do you think Mohr would like Puerto Ricans to learn from her writing?

4. Mohr was exposed to bigotry as a child. What effects do you think bigotry can have on people?

5. What qualities do you think the best writers and artists have? How are the qualities one needs for both professions similar?

SANDRA CISNEROS

Sandra Cisneros found her style, and her voice as a writer, when she realized that she had a unique story to tell. She then began to write about her childhood and about the Mexican American experience.

"**E**very time someone asks me to sign a book, I feel like laughing," says Sandra Cisneros (sees-NER-ohs). "It's so wacky. I was the girl with the C's and D's. I was the girl in the corner with the goofy glasses from Sears. I was the ugly kid in the class with the bad haircut, the one nobody would talk to. I was the one that never got picked to be in the play."

It was a long, hard trip from being a shy, poor, uncertain kid to becoming a nationally celebrated Latina[1] author. The difficulty of that journey has only made Cisneros more determined to tell others her story. One day, she hopes, her voice will be one of many explaining Latino life in this country.

Cisneros kept her writing a secret when she was a child in Chicago. "If you come from the neighborhood I come from, you had to hide everything that mattered to you. In the schools, teachers didn't expect us to be writers. I think they expected us to work in factories."

Cisneros's mother was the one who gave her the "fierce,"[2] or powerful, language, as she writes in the dedication to her book *Woman Hollering Creek.* "When she saw me with an open book in my hand, she saw that as work," Cisneros says. Born in 1954 into a family of six brothers, she was protected, sometimes too much so. "This is your sister. You must take care of her," Cisneros's father would say to his sons.

Her father had immigrated from Mexico. (See **Did You Know?** on page 20 for more information about immigration to the United States from Mexico.) Because Cisneros's father was very close to his mother in Mexico, the family often traveled back and forth from Mexico to the United States, changing

---

1. **Latina** (lah-TEE-na) *adj.* a woman from a Spanish-speaking country or with a cultural background from a Spanish-speaking country. A *Latina* is female. *Latino* refers to males or a group of males and females.
2. **fierce** (FEERS) *adj.* wild; intense

schools and homes. "It was very upsetting to me as a child," Cisneros says. "I do not remember making friends easily." Her defense was to haunt the library and become a people watcher. "People forget you are there and you can listen to their stories."

"My parents believed that we could rise above our circumstances,[3] and they taught us to believe in ourselves even when the education system did not." When Cisneros announced that she wanted to go to college, her parents agreed. Her mother thought she needed the skills to become independent. Her father thought she would be able to find a husband there.

She graduated from Loyola University in Chicago. Then she enrolled in the prestigious[4] Iowa Writers' Workshop. Once she arrived in Iowa, though, she felt alone in an alien world. "Nobody cared to hear what I had to say and no one listened to me even when I did speak." For Cisneros, it was a turning point, not because of what she learned in the classes but because of what she learned about herself.

One day her classmates were discussing their childhood homes. Cisneros had always been embarrassed by the shabby, cramped houses and apartments her family had lived in. At first, Cisneros thought that this discussion only proved that she didn't belong. "What could I know? My classmates were from the best schools in the country. They had been bred as hothouse[5] flowers. I was a yellow weed among the city's cracks.

"It was not until this moment when I separated myself, when I considered myself truly distinct,[6] when my writing acquired[7] a voice," she says. "That's when I decided I would write about something my classmates couldn't write about."

The result, published in 1984, was *The House on Mango Street,* a rich, poetic look at the world of Cisneros's youth through the

---

3. **circumstances** (SUR–kuhm-stahns-uhz) *n. pl.* situation
4. **prestigious** (preh-STIH-juhs) *adj.* important; famous
5. **hothouse** (HAHT-hows) *adj.* grown in a greenhouse
6. **distinct** (dihs-STIHNKT) *adj.* separate; unique
7. **acquired** (ah-KWEYERD) *v.* gained as one's own

eyes of another shy, uncertain girl. Cisneros has since been hailed by critics as "one of the most brilliant of today's young writers." The book has been reprinted several times.

The House on Mango Street describes longing for a better place to live. Mango Street is a place where people move to another street when you move in. The white people "who don't know any better come into our neighborhood scared. They think we're dangerous. They think we will attack them with shiny knives," she writes.

The success of this first novel should have been the beginning of a brilliant career for Cisneros, but it wasn't that easy. Even as the book gained admirers, Cisneros was having trouble paying the rent. She taught high-school dropouts, then worked as a college recruiter.[8] All the while she worked on her writing at night. She tried not to listen to her father, who told her to come home and stop living alone. He was angry and puzzled that his good Mexican daughter felt she had to move away from his protection.

In 1987, the year her first book of poetry, *My Wicked, Wicked Ways*, was published, she should have been rejoicing. Instead, she was in despair. Fellowships that allowed her to write had run out, and she couldn't find work. She convinced herself she was a failure.

Finally, Cisneros applied for and received another grant from the National Endowment for the Arts. That helped lift her spirits and gave her money on which to live. She also finally called Susan Bergholz, a literary agent who had been moved by Cisneros's writing and wanted to represent her in the publishing world. Bergholz had tried for years to contact Cisneros, but the writer, who was going through a period of self-doubt, hadn't returned Bergholz's calls. When she finally did, the agent took the first pages of the book of short stories that later became *Woman Hollering Creek* and sold the book to a major publisher, Random House. For Cisneros, selling the book meant

---

8. **recruiter** (rih-KROOT-uhr) *n.* someone who seeks new students

deadlines.[9] In the past, she had sometimes spent six months writing a single short story. The contract to publish the book meant that she had to produce an entire book within a few months. "There's nothing like a deadline to teach you discipline, especially when you've already spent your advance," Cisneros says.

The book was published to rave reviews. "Radiant," wrote *The New York Times Book Review.* "These stories invite us into the souls of characters."

Because the book was published by a major publishing house, Cisneros found herself becoming a celebrity. More people read her books. She could finally afford to write full time.

Cisneros now lives in San Antonio, Texas, as "nobody's mother and nobody's wife." Anyone who reads *The House on Mango Street* will understand Cisneros's deep affection for the house she bought in San Antonio. "This may sound corny, but one of the big blessings is that I have a house of my own—my own space." Cisneros's feelings for her home are understandable for someone who has painful memories of sharing too little space with too many family members.

Despite her success, Cisneros is passionate about remembering where she comes from. "I think about who I was, a quiet person who was never asked to speak in class and never picked for anything, and how I am finding that with words I have the power to make people listen, to make them think in a new way, to make them cry, to make them laugh. It's a powerful thing to make people listen to you."

> ***Did You Know?*** *Between 1880 and 1929, more than a million Mexicans immigrated to the United States, looking for a better life. During World War II, when there was a shortage of agricultural workers, the Mexican and United States governments created the Bracero program. Under this program, workers had*

---

9. **deadlines** (DEHD-leyenz) *n. pl.* dates by which something must be finished

temporary visas to the United States to work on farms. After the war, the program continued informally until 1964. During the period, about five million Mexicans worked on farms in the United States. The Bracero program had one negative result. It caused many U.S. citizens to believe that all Mexicans were unskilled farm laborers. In 1986, the U.S. Congress passed the Immigration and Reform Act. Mexicans who can prove they have been in this country since 1982 are granted resident status.

AFTER YOU READ

EXPLORING YOUR RESPONSES

1. Sandra Cisneros says that her mother gave her the "fierce" language she now uses in her books. What other important things can parents can give their children?

2. When Cisneros was in school, she often felt lonely. In what ways do people try to fit into a new group?

3. One of Cisneros's defenses to feeling left out was to become a people watcher. What can you learn by watching others?

4. Cisneros often writes about childhood. Think of another book you have read about childhood. Describe why you did or did not like the book.

5. As an adult, one of the things that means the most to Cisneros is having her own house. What do you most want to have as an adult?

UNDERSTANDING WORDS IN CONTEXT

Read the following sentences from the biography. Think about what each underlined word means. In your notebook, write what the word means as it is used in the sentence.

1. "My parents believed we could rise above our circumstances, and they taught us to believe in ourselves even when the education system did not."

2. She graduated from Loyola University in Chicago. Then she enrolled in the prestigious Iowa Writers' Workshop.

3. [Her classmates] "had been bred as hothouse flowers. I was a yellow weed among the city's cracks."

4. "It was not until this moment when I separated myself, when I considered myself truly distinct, when my writing acquired a voice," she says.

5. For Cisneros, selling the book meant <u>deadlines</u>. In the past, she had sometimes spent six months writing a single short story.

RECALLING DETAILS

1. Name three ways that Cisneros's mother encouraged her work.

2. How did Cisneros react to moving often as a child?

3. How did the Iowa Writers' Workshop help Cisneros develop as a writer?

4. Why wasn't the publication of Cisneros's book the start of an easy career as a writer?

5. Why was having a deadline helpful to Cisneros?

UNDERSTANDING INFERENCES

In your notebook, write two or three sentences from the biography that support each of the following inferences.

1. Cisneros's childhood affected her career.

2. Cisneros's mother helped her become a writer.

3. Cisneros rebelled against the protection of her brothers and her father.

4. Cisneros has faced discrimination in her life.

5. Cisneros would like to use her writing to reach other Latinos who feel left out as teenagers.

INTERPRETING WHAT YOU HAVE READ

1. Why do you think that Cisneros feels like laughing when someone asks her to sign a book?

2. Why do you think that Cisneros felt it was important for her to hide her writing when she was a child?

3. How does Cisneros's writing reflect her childhood?

4. How could being a people watcher as a child help Cisneros in her writing?

5. Why do you think that Cisneros feels it is important that her voice be heard in literature?

ANALYZING QUOTATIONS

Read the following quotation from the biography and answer the questions below.

> *"It was not until this moment when I separated myself, when I considered myself truly distinct, when my writing acquired a voice,"* she says. *"That's when I decided I would write about something my classmates couldn't write about."*

1. What do you think Cisneros meant when she said that "my writing acquired a voice"?

2. Why do you think it was important for Cisneros to separate herself from the other writers at the Iowa Writers' Workshop?

3. Why is it sometimes important for people to separate themselves from others?

THINKING CRITICALLY

1. Summarize what you think Cisneros's childhood was like.

2. How could growing up feeling protected, as Cisneros did, be a problem?

3. Why do you think Cisneros feels it is so important for her to remember what her early life was like?

4. What do you think led Cisneros to become a writer?

5. If Cisneros is very successful at making money from her books, do you think that will change her writing? Why or why not?

LUIS SANTEIRO

Cuban American writer Luis Santeiro poses with Elmo, a friend from "Sesame Street." Santeiro writes plays for adults, in addition to his Emmy award-winning work on "Sesame Street." His work for children and for adults shows that he writes not just about what he knows, but also about what he loves.

What kind of guy would consider Cookie Monster and Ernie his "best and oldest friends" in New York City? A guy who writes their lines, that's who. Luis Santeiro (loo–EES sahn–TAY–roh), who was born in Cuba in 1948, has been writing "Sesame Street" skits for 17 years. His affection for the Sesame Street gang hasn't kept him from other interests, though. Santeiro is also a celebrated playwright.

"Sesame Street" has provided a home for the writer that he still appreciates. "I love this place," Santeiro says of "Sesame Street." "You put on your comedy-writing hat and try to write for the child in you." For example, when Santeiro was young, he always wondered what adult parties were like. Based on that memory, he wrote a skit in which Big Bird longs to be invited to an adult party. "He makes such a fuss that they invite him," Santeiro says, "and he sees how boring adult parties are."

Santeiro has long been interested in the theater. At the age of about eight, he remembers watching a performance of *The Diary of Anne Frank* in a small theater in Havana, Cuba. "I instantly developed what would turn out to be a long love affair with the stage. I longed to be connected in some way with the making of all that magic."

As a child in Cuba, Santeiro was free to dream. He and his five younger brothers and sisters grew up with everything they wanted. Santeiro's great-grandfather was Gerardo Machado (heh–RAHR–doh mah–CHAH–doh), Cuba's president in the 1920s. (See **Did You Know?** on page 30 for more information about Cuba during the time Gerardo Machado was in office.) His family owned Crusellas (kroo–SEH–ahs), the Proctor & Gamble of Cuba, which manufactured items like shampoo and toothpaste. "We children didn't get on because we were looked after by separate nannies who didn't like each other," Santeiro says.

Like many who were in the upper classes in Cuba, the Santeiro family left the island in 1960 when the government began taking over private businesses, including the Santeiros' business. Fleeing with only what they could carry, the family left their financial security[1] behind and immigrated to Miami.

Life changed dramatically for the family in the United States. Instead of nannies, a huge house, and luxury,[2] there was a small three-bedroom house with bunk beds for the six children. Santeiro's father began selling encyclopedias and working for the Cuban Refugee[3] Center to support the family. Despite all this, Santeiro feels that the sense of having to depend on one another pulled the family together. "My mother says they were among the happiest days of her life."

After graduating from high school in Miami, Santeiro went to Villanova University, where he studied sociology.[4] Planning to work in film, he went to Syracuse University and earned a master's degree in communications. Then, as often happens, Santeiro's career took a slightly different turn. He got a job writing for "Carrascolendas," a children's show on public television in Texas. The title refers to an imaginary town in Texas, the setting for the show's mixture of songs and skits. The staff included everyone from Mexicans to Puerto Ricans to Cubans. "I loved the bizarre[5] quality of that crazy, mixed-up season in Texas," he says. "Before that, I not only wasn't aware of cultural clashes, I wasn't even particularly involved with my own cultural identity." Having to focus on the relationships in the script caused Santeiro to think about his heritage.

Next, Santeiro wrote a sample script for a proposed public television series about three generations of a Latino family. "I

1. **security** (sih-KYOO-ruh-tee) *n.* safety; protection
2. **luxury** (LUK-shuh-ree) *n.* something adding to pleasure but not necessary
3. **refugee** (reh-fyoo-GEE) *adj.* one who leaves one country to live in another country
4. **sociology** (soh-see-AH-luh-gee) *n.* the study of people and how they live together
5. **bizarre** (buh-ZAHR) *adj.* odd; fantastic; crazy

wrote a pilot for them and was told, 'This is what we've been looking for. You are the writer.' "

In many ways, the situation comedy[6] that Santeiro wrote mirrored his life. He described the clashes between the Americanized children and the parents and grandparents still firmly stuck in the attitudes of Cuba. The show, "¿Que Pasa, USA?," became an instant success. More important to Santeiro, though, was that the show offered a real look at the Cuban community in Miami. As he began working on it, "The program almost wrote itself. We all loved it. By creating this great family, we became a family." "¿Que Pasa, USA?," which still appears on public television, also won Santeiro his first Emmy award.

Then the writer landed a job in 1978 on "Sesame Street." He still writes for the regulars—Big Bird, Bert, Elmo, and the gang—as well as writing skits for guest stars, such as Linda Ronstadt and Gloria Estefan. (See the biography of Gloria Estefan on page 71.) Since his arrival, Santeiro has won eight Emmys for his work on the show.

With this television experience, Santeiro decided to try his luck in Los Angeles. CBS was interested in an idea he had for a television series. Santeiro found, though, that he disliked making network TV shows. Scripts[7] were changed, characters were changed, ideas were changed. It was, he says, one of the worst times of his life. "I was so unhappy. You feel you're getting the runaround. Nothing is on the level. There are these undercurrents.[8] And if you're going to be away from home and your friends, you shouldn't be miserable."

Finally, Santeiro was ready to get back to his first love, the theater. His first effort, *Our Lady of the Tortilla,* was written "because I was obsessed[9] with the theme of cultural shame," he explains. "Most children of immigrants in this country go

---

6. **situation comedy** (sih–chuh–WAY–shuhn KAH–muh–dee) a television comedy series that features the same characters each week
7. **scripts** (SKRIHPTS) *n. pl.* written texts of plays, movies, or TV shows
8. **undercurrents** (UHN–duhr–kuhr–uhnts) *n. pl.* hidden opinions or feelings
9. **obsessed** (uhb–SEHST) *v.* thought about constantly

through a process of becoming embarrassed by their ethnic backgrounds." In many immigrant families, as in this play, there are older people who refuse to accept new ways, to their children's dismay. In his play, Santeiro's young Latino character brings his Anglo girlfriend to meet his family, and tries to disguise his family's ethnicity. The play is "frenetically[10] funny" and "uproarious," the *New York Post* wrote. Since its premiere, *Our Lady of the Tortilla* has been performed throughout the United States.

Santeiro's third play, *The Lady from Havana,* is based on what happened when Santeiro's grandmother came to the United States in the 1970s. "There is not a wasted line in it," raved *The New York Times,* "and the author's good humor and warm feelings for his characters . . . flow right out into the audience."

Looking back at his plays, Santeiro realizes that he is dealing with issues that have been an important part of his life. "Some of my television work, and now all my plays, have involved Latin characters dealing in some way with life in this country. But I always hope that my work will have a crossover appeal—that non–Latins will find things in my plays with which they can identify, too."

Once an agent asked Santeiro why he only wrote about Latino issues. "I thought about this, and realized it wasn't just a matter of writing about what I knew. I was basically writing about what I loved. I came to this country at 13. My teenage years were consumed[11] with attempts to adapt and fit in. The imprint of those years was strong in me, and it is to them that I keep returning."

Despite his success as a playwright, Santeiro continues to write for "Sesame Street," a kind of home for the writer. "It disciplines me," he says. "It provides for me. It's a fun job and it gives me time to do all my other writing as well." Besides, a guy has to stay in touch with his best friends.

---

10. **frenetically** (fruh-NEHT-ihk-lee) *adv.* frantically; energetically
11. **consumed** (kuhn-SOOMD) *v.* fully occupied

Did You Know? *In the 1920s, Cuba's constitution was based on that of the United States. The country was also largely dominated by the United States after World War I, and economic conditions were poor. Gerardo Machado campaigned on a platform to change this situation, and was elected in 1924. The economy grew worse during his presidency, though. In 1933, he was overthrown by a Cuban army sergeant named Fulgencio Batista (fool-HEHN-seeoh bah-TEES-tah), who was supported by Cuba's army. Machado was then forced into exile.*

AFTER YOU READ

EXPLORING YOUR RESPONSES

1. Luis Santeiro often bases his "Sesame Street" skits on things he remembers from his childhood. What do you think would be a good idea for a "Sesame Street" skit?

2. When Santeiro was a child, he saw a play and knew he wanted to be connected to the theater. Write about something that has had a big influence on you.

3. Imagine that you are Luis Santeiro and you have just left your comfortable life behind to come to a new country and live in a tiny house with no money. What are your feelings?

4. Santeiro says that his teenage years were "consumed with attempts to fit in." What are some ways that teenagers try to fit in?

5. If you were going to create a pilot for a television show, what would it be about?

UNDERSTANDING WORDS IN CONTEXT

Read the following sentences from the biography. Think about what each underlined word means. In your notebook, write what the word means as it is used in the sentence.

1. Fleeing with only what they could carry, the family left their financial security behind and immigrated to Miami.

2. Instead of nannies, a huge house, and luxury, there was a small three-bedroom house with bunk beds for the six children.

3. Santeiro's father began selling encyclopedias and working for the Cuban Refugee Center to support the family.

4. "I loved the bizarre quality of that crazy, mixed-up season in Texas," he says.

5. "My teenage years were <u>consumed</u> with attempts to adapt and fit in."

RECALLING DETAILS

1. What began Luis Santeiro's lifelong love of the theater?
2. What was the difference between the way Santeiro's family lived in Cuba and the way they lived in the United States?
3. How did working on "Carrascolendas" affect Santeiro's life?
4. Why was Santeiro unhappy writing television scripts?
5. Why does Santeiro write about Latino issues?

UNDERSTANDING INFERENCES

In your notebook, write two or three sentences from the biography that support each of the following inferences.

1. Remembering his childhood helps Santeiro write for "Sesame Street."
2. Santeiro feels that people should be proud of both their first culture and U.S. culture.
3. Santeiro's experiences in this country are an important part of his plays.
4. Santeiro's work appeals to people of all cultures, not just Latinos.
5. Santeiro wants people to understand the immigrant experience through his plays.

INTERPRETING WHAT YOU HAVE READ

1. Do you think it was difficult or easy for Santeiro to adjust to the United States? Why?
2. How do you think having to depend on one another can "pull a family together"?

3. Santeiro says his play *Our Lady of the Tortilla* is about "cultural shame." Why might people be ashamed of their culture?

4. Why do you think "¿Que Pasa, U.S.A.?" was such a hit?

5. One reviewer mentions Santeiro's "warm feelings for the characters" in *The Lady from Havana*. Why would Santeiro have these feelings?

ANALYZING QUOTATIONS

Read the following quotation from the story and answer the questions below.

> *"It disciplines me," he says of "Sesame Street." "It provides for me. It's a fun job and it gives me time to do all my other writing as well."*

1. What do you think Santeiro means when he says that working for "Sesame Street" disciplines him?

2. What can you tell about Santeiro's ideas about his work from reading this quote?

3. What kind of job might you consider to be "fun"?

THINKING CRITICALLY

1. What qualities do you think Santeiro has that would make him a good playwright?

2. Do you think that Santeiro's writing would be the same if he had remained in Cuba? Why or why not?

3. How do you think that writing for television might be different from writing a play?

4. Santeiro wants his writing to appeal to people of all groups. How do you think a writer can accomplish this?

5. Santeiro uses plays to explain his culture to other people. What are some other ways in which a person could explain his or her culture to others?

JULIA ALVAREZ

Upon arriving in the United States, Julia Alvarez struggled to find words to express her feelings. She later found her writing style when she rediscovered the voices from her childhood in the Dominican Republic. Today, she uses those voices of home to create successful novels and collections of poetry.

"I'm the one who doesn't remember anything from that last day on the island because I'm the youngest and so the other three are always telling me what happened that last day," says Fifi. She is one of the characters in Julia Alvarez's (HOO-lee-ah AHL-vah-res) novel *How the Garcia Girls Lost Their Accents.* Fifi's voice is one that Alvarez understands. In many ways, what happened to this character mirrors her own experiences.

Like the family in her novel, Alvarez's family left the Dominican Republic in a panic in 1960 as the political situation on the island became dangerous. (See **Did You Know?** on page 39 for more information about the Dominican Republic in the 1960s.)

"Although I was raised in the Dominican Republic by Dominican parents in an extended Dominican family, mine was an American childhood," she says. To her family, the United States was the promised land.

"All my childhood I had dressed like an American, eaten American foods, and befriended American children. I had gone to an American school and spent most of the day speaking and reading English. At night, my prayers were full of blond hair and blue eyes and snow. . . . All my childhood I had longed for this moment of arrival. And here I was, an American girl, coming home at last."

For the new immigrant, life in the United States was different from what she had imagined. The family moved into a small apartment in New York City, which was a big change from the rambling family estate. Alvarez was shocked by the prejudice[1] she found. Some people in this blond, blue-eyed world called Alvarez and her three sisters names and told them to go back

---

1. **prejudice** (PREH-juh-duhs) *n.* suspicion or intolerance of other cultural, religious, or other groups

where they came from. After longing for the United States, Alvarez found that she missed her tropical homeland. She missed the recognition and respect her family had in the Dominican Republic. She also missed her cousins and the huge family she had left behind. Then there were the problems of fitting into a new world. The food was different, the streets could be rough, and instead of palms and grass, there was the concrete of New York City streets. "The feeling of loss caused a radical[2] change in me," she says. "It made me into an introverted[3] little girl.

"Imagine being from an Old World family in the Dominican Republic and suddenly being tossed into the crazy 1960s in America. It was a real jolt,"[4] Alvarez says. It was that jolt that started Alvarez writing. "I came here at ten years old and I lost my homeland. I felt that. I also lost my first language and had to learn another. I had to struggle to find words. Feeling alone, I began then to build an internal[5] world." Alvarez found comfort in books and in writing her feelings.

Since she began writing, Alvarez hasn't stopped. "I think if I had remained on the island I would not have become a writer. There is so much to do in my first country that it would be hard to choose the solitary life of a writer." When she returns, she often finds herself pitching in to help build something, or working with people who need help. When the need is so great, she says, it is hard to stay uninvolved.

Alvarez graduated from high school in New York, and then from Middlebury College in Vermont. She continued to write. "I had no models when I started out," she says. "There were very few women writers that I was taught in school, and no Latinas. I didn't know, for instance, that you could write a poem and use Spanish words. Whenever I did that, it was circled with a question mark."

---

2. **radical** (RAD-uh-kuhl) *adj.* extreme
3. **introverted** (IHN-truh-vurht-uhd) *adj.* someone whose attention is focused on himself or herself, not on the outside world
4. **jolt** (JOHLT) *n.* a sudden feeling of shock, surprise, or disappointment
5. **internal** (ihn-TUR-nuhl) *adj.* inside

After Alvarez earned her master's degree in creative writing at Syracuse University in New York, she was invited to Yaddo, an artists' colony where writers can work. Alvarez found herself wandering around, frustrated because she was unable to make her writing sound like that of the white writers she had been reading. "I was trying to sound like Yeats and Whitman, and I didn't have anything to say like them," she says.

Looking for someone to talk to, Alvarez wandered into the mansion that houses Yaddo. No one was there except the maids and the cooks. "I went downstairs and sat on the stool and talked to the cook and paged through her cookbook and started talking to her about cooking," Alvarez says. "I went back to the voices that I did hear—my mother, my aunts, maids, all talking about cooking and making beds and ironing and all that stuff." Alvarez turned those voices into poems that were eventually collected in her first book of poetry, titled *Homecoming*.

Finally, Alvarez began to make a living writing. Her first job after graduate school was with a Poets in the Schools program in Kentucky. "I'd pack up my little yellow Volkswagen and go from town to town," she says. "I'd only stay in each town for a few weeks, and I'd teach everywhere from grade schools and community colleges to prisons. All these people really knew about me was that I was somehow with the government. They'd ask me if I knew anything about their welfare checks. When I mentioned poetry, they thought I'd said 'poultry.' "

After that, Alvarez taught in California, Vermont, North Carolina, Illinois, and Delaware. In 1986, she published *Homecoming* and won a $20,000 grant from the National Endowment for the Arts. She used the money to spend a year writing in Charlotte, Vermont, and in the Dominican Republic. Living in her homeland, now as an adult, she came to see a more realistic vision of her homeland than the mythic[6] one of her childhood. For a while, she gave up writing, lived near a village, and helped build a school.

---

6. **mythic** (MIHTH-ihk) *adj.* imaginary

In 1988, Alvarez got a job at the college from which she had graduated, Middlebury. In 1991, she was given tenure there, which means a permanent place on the faculty. "My books and possessions, after all these years of traveling, have been scattered in the attics of so many friends' houses," she says. Those friends are still sending Alvarez's possessions to her Vermont home. "Things still seem to be arriving in the mail."

Life in Vermont is far from the tropical island life she led as a child, but Alvarez is happy there. The Vermont countryside gives her the peace she needs to write. "There's something about Vermont, both the landscape and the people, that feels settled and firmly rooted," she says. She is married to an eye surgeon, William Eichner. Their house is filled with colorful reminders of Latin America, such as bright rugs and wooden sculptures.

When her first novel, *How the Garcia Girls Lost Their Accents,* was published in 1991, the public loved it. The stories of the four Garcia girls are "tender, charming," wrote the *Washington Post.* "Simply wonderful writing," wrote *The Los Angeles Times.* "The novel becomes more powerful with each passing chapter."

Alvarez loves the ability to shut out the world and write in Vermont, but she would like to return to the Dominican Republic someday to live. "My husband and I are thinking of buying some land on the island and maybe starting a clinic there," she adds. "I lead such a privileged life here."

It has been a long journey for Alvarez, from the relative wealth of her life on the island, to the problems of being a poor immigrant, to the comfort and peace of the remote Vermont countryside where Alvarez lives. But the Dominican Republic continues to draw Alvarez. "When I go back I see the problems that are there. This is a Third World country we are talking about. I feel a mandate[7] to pay back and serve," Alvarez says. "What is a life for?"

---

7. **mandate** (MAN–dayt) *n.* a command

***Did You Know?** The political history of the Dominican Republic has been stormy in this century. In the 1930s, Rafael Trujillo Molina (rah-FAY-ehl troo-HEE-yoh moh-LEE-nah) began a corrupt dictatorship that ended in 1961 when he was assassinated. In 1962, Juan Bosch was elected in a democratic election, but he was overthrown a year later. Civil war broke out in 1965 between those who supported Bosch and those who opposed him. A year later, elections were held and Joaquín Balaguer (hohah-KEEN bah-lah-GHER) defeated Bosch. Balaguer held office until 1978, and made progress in bringing stability to the country.*

AFTER YOU READ

EXPLORING YOUR RESPONSES

1. When Alvarez came to the United States, some people called her names. Why do you think people do this?

2. When Alvarez began writing, she had "no models." Do you think it is important to have a model? Explain.

3. Vermont, where Alvarez now lives, is very different from her first home. What might be the good and bad points about moving so far away from your first home?

4. Alvarez often writes about what happened to her. What character in a book or movie are you most like? Explain.

5. Alvarez still wants to go back and help her native country. How could you help other people?

UNDERSTANDING WORDS IN CONTEXT

Read the following sentences from the biography. Think about what each underlined word means. In your notebook, write what the word means as it is used in the sentence.

1. Alvarez was shocked by the prejudice she found. Some people in this blond, blue-eyed world called Alvarez . . . names.

2. The food was different, the streets could be rough, and instead of palms and grass, there was the concrete of New York City streets. "The feeling of loss caused a radical change in me."

3. "Imagine being from an Old World family in the Dominican Republic and suddenly being tossed into the crazy 1960s in America. It was a real jolt," Alvarez says.

4. Living in her homeland, now as an adult, she came to see a more realistic vision of her homeland than the mythic one of her childhood.

5. "I feel a <u>mandate</u> to pay back and serve," Alvarez says. "What is a life for?"

RECALLING DETAILS

1. Why did the Alvarez family leave the Dominican Republic?

2. How was being in the United States different from what Alvarez expected?

3. Why does Alvarez feel that she would not have become a writer if she had stayed in the Dominican Republic?

4. Why was Alvarez having trouble writing at Yaddo?

5. Why would Alvarez consider returning to the Dominican Republic to live?

UNDERSTANDING INFERENCES

In your notebook, write two or three sentences that support each of the following inferences.

1. As a child, Alvarez believed that life in the United States was better than life in her native country.

2. Writing was an important way for Alvarez to learn to cope and make herself happy in the United States.

3. Alvarez had to find her own voice before she became a successful writer.

4. Alvarez's writing appeals to a variety of people.

5. Alvarez finds it easiest to write when she is settled and away from other people.

INTERPRETING WHAT YOU HAVE READ

1. Why do you think that Alvarez feels it is important to write about her experiences as a Latina?

2. Why do you think that Alvarez kept writing, even though she had no role models?

3. How did the maids and cooks at Yaddo help Alvarez find something to write about?

4. How might returning to the Dominican Republic as an adult affect Alvarez's writing?

5. Why do you think that Alvarez bases much of her writing on her experience?

ANALYZING QUOTATIONS

Read the following quotation from the biography and answer the questions below.

> "I came here at ten years old and I lost my homeland. I felt that. I also lost my first language and had to learn another. I had to struggle to find words. Feeling alone, I began then to build an internal world."

1. What do you think Alvarez means when she says that she began to build an internal world?

2. Do you think that Alvarez lost her homeland? Explain.

3. What do you think would be the hardest thing about moving to a new country?

THINKING CRITICALLY

1. Describe the world you think Alvarez expected to find in the United States.

2. Why do you think that Alvarez responded to her disappointment by writing?

3. Before she went to Yaddo, why do you think Alvarez tried to make her writing sound like that of the writers she had been reading?

4. Do you think Alvarez will continue to write if she moves to the Dominican Republic? Explain.

5. What are some advantages and disadvantages of moving to a new country when you are a child?

TATO LAVIERA

Tato Laviera's poetry speaks of being Puerto Rican, African American, and "other" in a largely white society. He believes that poetry can help people share, and better understand, the experiences and feelings of others.

Flying to New York City from Puerto Rico in 1960 when he was nine, Tato Laviera (TAH-toh lah-vee-ER-ah) thought everyone in the United States was white. "I thought I would be the only black person there," he recalls. When Laviera and his family arrived at the airport in their new country, his aunt met them. "Don't hang around with black people," she warned him. "I looked at my skin," Laviera says, "And I said, 'But *I'm* black.'" There were Puerto Rican and black gangs, Laviera found out later, which led to his aunt's warning. This was the first of many confusions Laviera felt in his new home.

The Laviera family moved to New York City's Lower East Side. The family lived alongside African Americans, Jews, Chinese, Cubans, Arabs, Irish, Greeks, Italians—a diverse group of people. Like their neighbors, the Laviera family had little money, but his sister became a well-liked hairstylist and his mother was an excellent dressmaker. The family was close. "There was always a sense of community there. My sister was very popular, and we had a lot of extended family.[1]"

During his first year in the United States, Laviera feels that "The most important thing that happened to me is that my name changed. My real name is Jesus Abraham (heh-SOOS AH-brah-hahm) Laviera. When I went to Catholic school, they cut my name with a machete.[2] I became Abraham." Although Jesus is a common name in Mexico and South America, Laviera couldn't be called Jesus, the nuns told him, because they always bowed to Jesus. "I didn't realize until much later how much that meant, to cut my name, I realized later it was cutting off my identity."

In Puerto Rico "I was the smartest student," Laviera says. That changed in a school in which he could barely understand

---

1. **extended family** (ihk-STEHND-uhd FAM-uh-lee) a family that includes relatives such as grandparents, cousins, uncles, and aunts
2. **machete** (muh-SHEH-tee) *n.* a large, heavy knife

what was being said. "One time a sister didn't just give me an F. She gave me a Z. I tried to turn it around and tell my mother it was an N."

Later that same year, "the second most important thing happened to me. I won the spelling bee in the school." The winner of that contest would represent the school at the city-wide spelling bee. The people in charge of the school didn't know what to do. "They told me I couldn't represent the school. They knew I didn't know English." They tried to talk Laviera out of competing. He stubbornly refused to back out. "I told them I wouldn't win, but I wouldn't be the first person out, either." The school officials gave in. Laviera spent hours studying flash cards with spelling words. True to his word, he didn't win—and he wasn't the first one out.

In 1967, when he was 16, Laviera wrote his first poem. He was looking out a window when something caught his eye across the street. "There was this kid in an abandoned building. He was on his hands and knees, no shoes. When I went down, he had disappeared. I wrote a poem right there, on a paper bag." A few minutes later, a well-known Puerto Rican painter came by. "He read what I wrote, and he took the poem with him. Three hours later, he came back with a painting he gave me." Laviera came to think that "that kid was my muse,[3] and I would never see him again." Laviera never did see the boy again. He has also not stopped writing.

By the time he was 12 years old, just three years after he came to the United States, Laviera had begun baby-sitting neighborhood children after school. Laviera turned that baby-sitting service into an after-school program for seventh and eighth graders. It grew and Laviera moved it to the basement of a housing project.

After his rocky beginning at school, Laviera graduated from high school as an honor student and enrolled at Brooklyn College. His success at teaching kids in the after-school program

---

3. **muse** (MYOOZ) *n.* a source of inspiration

led to a job at Rutgers University in New Jersey teaching basic writing skills for incoming students in a program called the University of the Streets. Soon he was the program's director. "I got on this big ego trip. I was a big thing for the community." After that heady experience, "My whole thing was community service." He began as associate director of a local association for community services. Three years later, he was running the program. Its budget had gone from $500,000 to $3,500,000 a year.

Then, in 1979, he met Nicholás Kanellos (kah–NEH-yohs) and read him some of his poetry. Kanellos was struck by Laviera's strong voice as a poet. His viewpoint was not just Puerto Rican and not just New York. It was Nuyorican (noo–yohr-EE-kuhn). It explained the experience of a Puerto Rican in New York City. It talked about being black, about being Latino, about being "other" in a largely white society. Laviera's poems are written in Spanish and English and sometimes in both, in a kind of "Spanglish."

His poems are also strongly influenced by the music of Puerto Rico. (See **Did You Know?** on page 48 for more information about Puerto Rican music.)

Kanellos was so taken by Laviera's work that he had Laviera collect his work into a book. These poems, called *La Carreta*[4] *Made a U-Turn,* became the first book published by Kanellos's Arte Público Press. The poems deal with the problems that poor Puerto Ricans face in New York City. They are poems about cold, hunger, high rents, unemployment, and the problems of Puerto Rican women.

"That it was the first book in our history was either fate[5] or blind luck," writes Kanellos. "That Arte Público Press would have as its first and greatest ambassador such a dynamic[6] and beloved figure as Tato Laviera was again incredibly fortunate."

---

4. **carreta** (kah–RREH-tah) *n.* Spanish for *cart*
5. **fate** (FAYT) *n.* the belief that events will happen in a certain way
6. **dynamic** (deye-NA-mihk) *adj.* having a lot of energy

This publishing company is now the most important publisher of Latino works in the United States.

After Laviera's book was published, he quit his job in social services to become a poet. Many people would worry about giving up a stable[7] job to make a living as a poet, but Laviera had no trouble making his decision—or making a living. Laviera sees himself as being in the tradition of Jorge Brandon, a Puerto Rican poet in New York City. "He is the elder poet of our community," Laviera says. "He is a hero to us all." Brandon told Laviera that he couldn't just write poems. "He said you have to memorize your poetry, if it's going to go anywhere. You have to know how to declaim[8] it." That declaiming has become a central part of Laviera's work. He can hold a group of people spellbound by reciting his poetry.

The response to Laviera's first book was startling. His ability to put words to the experience of Puerto Ricans in New York made him a hero in New York and gained him national attention. A year after the book was released, Tato Laviera was in the White House meeting then-President Jimmy Carter at a gathering of the nation's poets.

What has helped Laviera make a living as a poet is his belief that poetry is meant to be performed as well as read. Since the publication of his first book, Laviera has constantly toured colleges, reading his poetry and giving workshops on writing. "I get paid very well when I visit colleges," he says. "The reason is that I don't like to go just to recite poetry. I like to go spend the whole day there. I do a writing workshop, a dramatic workshop, I meet with the student leaders, and I also ask a community group to co-sponsor the visit."

Since his first book, Laviera has published four other books of poetry. He is the best-selling Latino poet in the United States. Even more impressive is that all of his books are still in print. Most poetry is published, sells a few copies, and is never heard of

---

7. **stable** (STAY-buhl) *adj.* steady; secure
8. **declaim** (dih-KLAYM) *v.* to recite a poem or other work in a dramatic way

again. Besides his poetry, Laviera has also written eight plays that have been produced.

When he sits down to write, Laviera recites to himself a poem that he wrote for his mentor,[9] Jorge Brandon. The poem starts like this.

> poetry is an outcry, love, affection,
> a sentiment,[10] a feeling, an attitude,
> a song.

Did You Know? *Tato Laviera's poetry is deeply influenced by the popular rhythms of Puerto Rican music. Most important are the Puerto Rican plenas (PLAY-nahs). The influence of African slaves (brought to the island by Spanish colonists) is clear in these songs, which are accompanied by hand-held percussion instruments and made for dancing. These instruments include gourd rattles called maracas and the guiro (WEE-roh), a long, hollow gourd played with a stick.*

---

9. **mentor** (MEHN-tawr) *n.* a trusted guide or teacher
10. **sentiment** (SEHN-tuh-muhnt) *n.* a thought that is influenced by emotion

AFTER YOU READ

EXPLORING YOUR RESPONSES

1. Imagine that someone changed your name. How might you react?

2. Laviera wrote his first poem when he was moved by the sight of a poor child, and he has been writing since. How did you start doing something that you enjoy?

3. Tell about your mentor, or someone who has had a positive effect on your life.

4. Laviera quit a job with a regular salary to become a poet. Would you quit a job with a good salary to do something you love? Explain your answer.

5. Laviera writes about being a Nuyorican. If you were a poet, what would you most want people to learn through your poetry?

UNDERSTANDING WORDS IN CONTEXT

Read the following sentences. Think about what each underlined word means. In your notebook, write what the word means as it is used in the sentence.

1. The family was close. "There was always a sense of community there. My sister was very popular, and we had a lot of extended family."

2. Laviera came to think that "that kid was my muse, and I would never see him again." Laviera never did see the boy again. He has also not stopped writing.

3. "That Arte Público Press would have as its first and greatest ambassador such a dynamic and beloved figure as Tato Laviera was again incredibly fortunate."

4. "He said you have to memorize your poetry, if it's going to go anywhere. You have to know how to <u>declaim</u> it."

5. When he sits down to write, Laviera recites to himself a poem that he wrote for his <u>mentor</u> Jorge Brandon.

RECALLING DETAILS

1. Describe the neighborhood in which Laviera lived in New York City.

2. What did Laviera say was the most important thing that happened to him during his first year in the United States?

3. How did Laviera start writing poetry?

4. How did Laviera become involved in community service?

5. What does Laviera do in addition to writing poetry?

UNDERSTANDING INFERENCES

In your notebook, write two or three sentences from the biography that support each of the following inferences.

1. Laviera's first year in school was difficult.

2. Laviera writes about what he knows.

3. Several people helped Laviera succeed in his poetry career.

4. Jorge Brandon's influence has shaped Laviera's work.

5. To become successful as a poet, Laviera did more than just publish books.

INTERPRETING WHAT YOU HAVE READ

1. What do you think was the hardest part of moving to the United States for Laviera? Explain your answer.

2. Why do you think that Laviera refused to let someone else represent the school at the spelling bee?

3. Who do you think had the most influence on Laviera's career? Explain your answer.

4. Why do you think Laviera thinks declaiming his work is so important?

5. Why do you think that Laviera recites the poem he wrote for Jorge Brandon before he begins writing?

ANALYZING QUOTATIONS

Read the following quotation from the biography and answer the questions below.

> "He said you have to memorize your poetry, if it's going to go anywhere. You have to know how to declaim it."

1. What do you think it means to have poetry "go anywhere"?

2. Do you think that Laviera believes what Brandon said? Why or why not?

3. Do you prefer reading or having someone read to you? Why?

THINKING CRITICALLY

1. Why do you think that Laviera has chosen to devote his life to poetry?

2. What qualities do you think Laviera has shown in his life that make him a successful poet?

3. Why do you think Laviera has become the best-selling Latino poet in the United States?

4. How do you think poetry could be influenced by music?

5. Laviera explains his world by writing poetry. In what form would you explain your world?

CULTURAL CONNECTIONS

Thinking About What People Do

1. Compare two of the writers from this unit and explain how their childhoods shaped their writing. Relate at least one specific incident from each of the writers you select.

2. Work with a partner to write a letter to one of the writers you read about. Think of some important events or turning points in your writer's life. Decide with your partner which one was the most significant event. In your letter, write about your impressions of this event.

3. Describe the support that at least two subjects had from members of their families. Tell how this support influenced their careers.

Thinking About Culture

1. You have been introduced to writers from various cultural backgrounds in this unit. How did their heritage prove to be an advantage for two of the people you read about? Describe the similarities and differences of the two writers you select.

2. All of the subjects of these biographies write about their cultural heritage. Which of these authors writes about experiences that are common to people from all heritages? Give examples from the unit.

3. Explain how discrimination, or the negative attitude of another person, might force someone to work harder to achieve his or her goal. Give examples from the selections in this unit or from your own experience.

Building Research Skills

Work with a partner to complete the following activity.

Choose one of the subjects in this unit whose life or work interests you. Imagine that this person is scheduled to appear as a guest on a TV talk show and that you will interview him or her. Write some questions that you will use in your interview. You might want to include questions such as these:

Hint: The Bibliography at the back of this book lists articles and books to help you begin your research.

☆ Why did you choose the particular style of writing that you did?

☆ What schooling helped you prepare for your career?

☆ Do you use musical or artistic qualities in your writing?

Hint: As you reread the biographies, write some notes to help you remember those topics or details that you want to find out more about later.

☆ How would you advise a young writer?

☆ In your opinion, what is the single most important factor in being a successful writer?

Next, go to the library and find articles or other information about your subject to help you answer your questions. You might also look for works written by him or her.

Hint: Watch a TV news panel, such as Meet the Press, to see a good model of interview questions.

Share your findings with your class. You might wish to stage an interview, with a partner acting as the writer and you as the interviewer.

Extending Your Studies

MUSIC   **Your task:** *To learn about a Latin American country through its folk songs and folktales.*

Folk songs usually tell about the traditions or values of a country or region. Many honor a real or imaginary hero.

The subjects of the biographies in this unit have many different homelands. With a partner, choose one of the countries that you have learned about. Go to the library and find a songbook, storybook, or recording from this country. Research some facts about the country in encyclopedias and other reference materials.

Learn to sing one of the folk songs you find, or practice reciting a poem or short folktale from that country. Use some of the ideas and information from your research to write a brief introduction to the song or poem you have chosen. Perhaps you can find an illustration or photograph about your song or poem. Make sure your introduction includes accurate details of your selected country. You might mention national colors, holidays, flags, costumes, or foods.

Perform your song, poem, or folktale with your partner for the class or for a special cultural heritage program. You may enjoy videotaping or recording your classmates' acts.

LANGUAGE ARTS   **Your task:** *To write a skit and perform it for the class.* You read about Luis Santeiro's work in writing plays and television scripts for children. A *skit* is a short dramatic work, or a part of a longer play. Several *characters* are involved in the skit's *plot*, which is the story that is told about the characters. The *setting* is the location in which the skit takes place.

Work with two or three partners to create a simple story that children might enjoy. Write an outline of the story, being sure that you have written a clear beginning, middle, and end.

Write some *dialogue*, or conversation, for the characters in your skit. You may also include a *narrator* to provide background or a framework for your story. With your partners, finish a draft of your skit. Then assign parts and act it out. You may decide to revise lines to make your characters sound like real people.

When your skit is in final form, perform it for your class. You might also make copies of your script for a class drama collection.

SOCIAL STUDIES **Your task:** *To write a time line of some events in the 1930s.* You learned in this unit that Nicholasa Mohr's family emigrated to this country during the Great Depression in the 1930s. Find some newspaper accounts or encyclopedia articles about the immigration of one group of people to the United States at this time. Use the card catalog at the library and the *Readers' Guide to Periodical Literature* to locate information. Make a time line to show some significant U.S. history events of the 1930s in chronological, or time, order. Share information with your classmates and add it to your time line.

WRITING WORKSHOP

When you write the story of your own life, that story is called your **autobiography**. Writing about yourself may not seem like a difficult task. After all, who knows you better than you know yourself? Even so, autobiographical writing can be a challenge.

In this lesson, you will write an **autobiographical essay** about one event in your life. This event should demonstrate something about your character or personality. In your essay, you will share your thoughts with your classmates. Another student will assist you in editing your writing. Having a classmate's point of view will help you ensure that your work makes sense and is enjoyable to read.

PREWRITING

Before you start to write your essay, think about your topic, organize your thoughts, and take notes. The first step in the writing process is called **prewriting**. You can use many different prewriting strategies to get started. Here are two suggestions:

Brainstorming: On a blank sheet of paper, make a chart with three columns. Label the columns *Who*, *What*, and *Where*. Your paper might look like this:

Who	What	Where

Jot down the names of people you know, events you've experienced, and places you've visited. You may choose friends, family members, or persons in your neighborhood or school. You may think of major events, such as moving to a new town, or small ones, such as doing a special favor for someone.

Work quickly to fill your columns with as many items as you remember. Do not worry about the spelling or the order of the names. Let your thoughts wander and write whatever comes to mind. When you fill your chart, you will have many different ideas for your essay.

Asking questions: Explore your topic further by asking yourself questions about it. Choose *one* of the ideas from your brainstorming list and write this topic at the top of a blank piece of paper. Then list as many questions as possible about your topic. As you write your list, think about what these questions reveal about you. Here are some questions to help you get started:

☆ What happened?

☆ How old was I?

☆ Who else was involved?

☆ Why is this location important to me?

☆ What did I learn from this person or event?

☆ What does this person mean to me now?

☆ How did I react to the visit or incident?

Look over your questions and choose the ones that are most appropriate to your topic. Answer some of the questions and fill in personal details that will help your reader see the real you.

Organizing: Next, put your ideas in a clear and logical order. You will probably write about your topic in *chronological order*, that is, in the sequence in which the events happened. Arrange your notes in the order in which you will use them.

DRAFTING

Now you can begin writing, or **drafting**, your autobiographical essay. You may want to keep the following strategies in mind as you write:

Use dialogue: Using the actual words of people adds life and variety to your writing. Choose words that show your personality and that of others, if you can.

Use colorful language: Include vivid details that will appeal to your readers' senses: sight, hearing, smell, touch, and taste. Try to surprise your readers at the beginning and keep that interest. Be honest and open about yourself and the things you are describing.

Tell an exciting story: Keep the pace moving. Do not stop to make your draft perfect. You will check for word usage and spelling errors later.

REVISING

Put your essay aside for a day or two. Then, with the help of another student who will act as your editor, evaluate and **revise** your work. See the directions for writers and student editors below.

Directions for Writers: Read your work aloud. Listen to the way the words flow. Ask yourself the following questions:

☆ Is my writing clear?

☆ Are the ideas in a logical order?

☆ Do all sentences make sense?

☆ Did I include interesting details?

☆ Have I drawn a colorful picture of my event so that my readers can see it in their minds?

☆ Have I shown my readers why this event was important to me?

Make notes for your next draft or revise your work before you give it to a student editor. Then ask the student editor to read your essay. Listen carefully to his or her suggestions. If they seem helpful, use them to improve your writing when you revise your work.

Directions for Student Editors: Read the work carefully and respectfully, keeping in mind that your purpose is to help the writer do his or her best work. Remember that an editor should always make positive, helpful comments that point to specific parts of the essay. After you read the work, use the following questions to help you direct your comments:

☆ What did I like most about the essay?

☆ What would I like to know more about?

☆ Can I see the scene or event clearly in my mind?

☆ Do I understand what the event means to the writer?

PROOFREADING

When you are satisfied that your work says what you want it to say, **proofread** it for errors in spelling, punctuation, capitalization, and grammar. Then make a neat, final copy of your autobiographical essay.

PUBLISHING

After you revise and proofread your autobiographical essay, you are ready to **publish** it. Design a title page that states the title of your essay and includes your name as the author. Then personalize your work with a graphic decoration or illustration to show the real you. Display your essay as part of a class Who's Who.

LATINOS IN FINE ARTS AND PERFORMANCE

How do you express your creativity? Achievement in the fine and performing arts often requires hard work, high energy, and strong willpower, as well as talent. The five Latinos you will read about in this unit have earned recognition in their fields. How have each of these artists taken steps toward their goals?

Mexican American artist **Judith Baca** (BAH-keh) paints murals that deliver strong messages of peace and cooperation. She believes that "the power of ideas can move around the world."

Celebrated Latina singer **Gloria Estefan** (es-TEF-ahn) performs with her heart and her heritage in mind: "[My music is] reflective of my cultural mix of Cuban American . . . a tribute to my homeland, one side of my roots."

"Whenever you give from a feeling inside, you receive back a tremendous sense of self-esteem," says Mexican American actor **Edward James Olmos** (OHL-mohs) about his life and his work for Latino causes.

"Greatness depends on taking risks," according to Cuban American ballet dancer **Fernando Bujones** (boo-HOH-nes). Enormous personal drive and hard work have led to his success as a performer and choreographer.

As an actor and director, **Miriam Colón** (koh-LOHN) brings Latino theater to the streets of New York City: "[We are] a Puerto Rican group energizing something in the community. We wanted to emphasize Puerto Rican culture."

After reading the biographies in this unit, think about the quotations above. Decide if each statement gives a clear picture of the individual or if you would choose a different quotation.

JUDITH BACA

Mexican American artist Judith Baca decided to create art that speaks to people like her grandmother and others in her community. Her murals focus on creating a sense of unity among cultural groups from around the world.

Judith Baca told the Los Angeles teenagers to hold out their hands. When they did, she said, "We need every hand here. We have nine weeks and we have 350 feet of wall. It's these hands that will make [this mural]."

Nine weeks later Judith Baca and her crew had turned a wall that had been covered with graffiti into a huge painting. Larger-than-life people from the neighborhood seemed to say that this wasn't just a poor neighborhood. It was a place with life, and dignity.

The murals "were powerful, and they were strong, and they were political," Baca says. "They talked about who those people were, what they cared about, and what they were mad about." In a few short years, and with a lot of help, Baca had changed the way her world looked.

Judith Baca was born in Los Angeles in 1946 and grew up in a household of women. She didn't know her father, who was a musician. Judith, her grandmother, mother, and two aunts lived together. She was raised mostly by her grandmother while her mother worked in a tire factory. "It was a strong, wonderful, matriarchal[1] household," Baca says. "I was everybody's child."

When she was six, her mother married Clarence Ferrari and moved with Baca to Pacoima, California. She missed her grandmother and the Spanish-speaking world of South Central L.A. "When I went into the school system, I was *forbidden* to speak Spanish. I did not speak English. I remember being in rooms with people speaking this other language. I didn't understand the words they were saying, but I knew clearly that they were saying I was less than they were because I didn't speak

---

1. **matriarchal** (may-tree-AHR-kuhl) *adj.* a type of family that is headed by a woman

their language. . . . I thought to myself, they're not going to be able to do this to me. I'm going to learn what they're saying."

It was a time, she says, "when everybody was working very hard at just being American. Everyone should all blend in. All separate ethnic groups should just disappear and become American."

Her mother believed that, too. She was a second-generation Chicana, or Mexican American. "My mother worked on getting me to speak English without an accent," Baca recalls. "That was real important to her because that accent was an identification. She would have liked me to blend in if I could have, although at this point in her life she's very proud that I didn't."

Baca's mother also pushed Baca to study. "Like a lot of immigrant people, she felt that education was the key if I was to avoid suffering the kinds of things she had suffered." The only thing that saved Baca from a miserable school experience was her talent for art. Often while the rest of the class worked, she was allowed to paint.

After graduating from high school, Baca went to the University of California in Northridge. She was married during her first year, a marriage that lasted six years. It was a time of conflict for her. "I was encouraged to be fairly independent," she says, but "I also had all those other messages. Get married, have children, do all that stuff. But I wanted to be an artist. My family didn't want me to be an artist because it was a crazy thing to do."

Baca also felt alone in college. "Looking across the campus, I would never see a Mexican or a black person or anybody of color. The moment I left my community to go to college, I was isolated from my own people because not that many of them went to college. I was isolated from any sense of my own culture in the university system."

Baca's family was puzzled when they saw the abstract[2] work that she had done in college. "When I showed her my work, my

---

2. **abstract** (ab-STRAKT) *adj.* a type of art that does not attempt to picture something as it is in life

grandmother said to me, 'What is this? What's it for?' It was clear to me that somehow I had been encouraged not to be who I was, [but] to use Western European art as my model."

Baca reflected long and hard about her family's reaction. "I thought 'These are the people I really know and care about. I love these people, and I really want to make them understand.' " Baca decided to make her art speak to people like her grandmother. She would skip the art galleries. "I thought to myself, if I get my work into galleries, who will go there? People in my family had never been to a gallery in their entire lives."

So Baca took to the streets. She worked as an art teacher at the high school from which she graduated. Then she began working for the city, helping teenagers learn about art. The idea of doing murals with them came easily. Writing on the walls was already a part of life on the street. "You could read a wall and learn everything you needed to know about that community." The murals would also help convince these people that the community belonged to them. Other than through graffiti, Baca explains, the people did not feel as if they were a part of their landscape. They hadn't built these buildings, they had no identification with them. Murals helped change that. They incorporated[3] a style of expression that was familiar to the kids—graffiti—with stories about the neighborhood, all turned into art.

Baca assembled 20 teenagers from four different gangs to work on a mural. "I said I wanted to form a mural team. Pretty soon I had a number of people who began to hang with me, who trusted me and would do anything I asked them to do. At that point nobody knew what a mural was," she recalls. "I had to explain that we were going to do a big picture on the wall."

Baca's first murals helped bridge the gap between the immigrants and their children. "Their parents hated them for not being good Mexican kids and thought they had gotten completely out of control. It's that old country–new country stuff," she says. "But when the parents saw their kids doing

---

3. **incorporated** (ihn-KAWR-puh-ray-tuhd) *v.* blended or combined into

something positive, connections among the family members began to develop again."

The city was delighted at her results. Baca was "putting up murals with kids who had run directors out of neighborhood centers. The city let me do my own thing."

After that first mural, someone gave Baca a book about Los Tres Grandes—the three famous Mexican muralists Diego Rivera, David Alfaro Siqueiros, and José Clemente Orozco. (See **Did You Know?** on page 67 for more information about these Mexican muralists.) In the mid-1970s, Baca went to Mexico to study mural painting.

In 1974, Baca decided to expand her mural project to the entire city of Los Angeles. Getting the money and the permission took months. "The most important skill I've had to develop in this work is to be able to deal with people in City Hall, then jump in my car, drive ten miles to the East Side, change into boots and jeans, and go sit on the curb with the kids. It was truly an amazing experience," Baca remembers. "We did 250 murals and hired over 1,000 people. It wore me out."

Baca left the project in the late 1970s to do her own work. *The Great Wall* was the most ambitious project she did during those years. It was a mural a half-mile long that told, in painting, a history of the people of Los Angeles. Even this, though, was not a project she did alone. When painting murals, you have to work with others, she believes. "It isn't like other art forms you might be able to accomplish by yourself."

At the same time she was working on *The Great Wall*, Baca began SPARC (Social and Public Art Resource Center) in 1976 to encourage public art. It is now an internationally recognized center that helps people learn about or aid public art, such as the murals Baca and the teenagers did in Los Angeles.

In 1987, Baca began an even grander project. It is called *World Wall: A Vision of the Future Without Fear.* The themes of the mural—peace and cooperation—came from talking with artists all over the world. "My idea was that what we had learned with the interracial[4] work in Los Angeles could be applied to an international scope, from the neighborhood to the global," she says. Baca now felt that she could help create a sense of unity among cultural groups from around the world.

The first discussions about the work were difficult. "It occurred to me later that it was not imagining destruction that was so hard to us but rather imagining peace," she says. "If we cannot imagine peace as an active concept,[5] how can we ever hope for it to happen?"

By 1994, Baca had completed four of the seven panels of the mural, each 10 by 30 feet. At this point, the mural traveled to the former Soviet Union and then to Finland. In each of the seven countries the mural will visit, an artist completes a panel for the work. By the end of its journey, the mural will contain 14 panels.

Raising money for this project has not been easy. She feels strongly, however, that this project is important to the world. "As artists, we have the power of spreading ideas, and this is a way in which the power of ideas can move around the world."

It is that power of ideas—ideas of peace, of different races understanding and respecting one another—that has inspired Baca. Since those first murals, it is a power she has used to try to bring the world into harmony.

> *Did You Know? In the 1920s, the Mexican muralists Diego Rivera (ree-VEH-rah), José Clemente Orozco (oh-ROHS-koh), and David Alfaro Siqueiros (see-keh-EE-rohs) stunned the world with bold, passionate art that focused on the social struggles of the Mexican people. Unlike most European art, these works told life and death stories that were painted on walls, not canvases. Today murals are a powerful form not only for artists in Mexico, but also for many Latino artists in this country.*

4. **interracial** (ihn-tuhr-RAY-shuhl) *adj.* involving or concerned with members of different heritages
5. **concept** (KAHN-sehpt) *n.* idea

AFTER YOU READ

EXPLORING YOUR RESPONSES

1. Do you think graffiti should be illegal or should it be a legal form of expression? Explain.

2. What advice would you give to someone who was discriminated against because he or she could not speak English?

3. The parents of the students who were working on the murals began to connect with their children again after seeing their art. What are some other ways that children can make connections with their parents?

4. To create a mural, many people work together. What projects have you worked on that also require many people?

5. Baca believes that murals can spread ideas around the world. In what other ways can ideas move around the world?

UNDERSTANDING WORDS IN CONTEXT

Read the following sentences from the biography. Think about what each underlined word means. In your notebook, write what the word means as it is used in the sentence.

1. She was raised mostly by her grandmother while her mother worked in a tire factory. "It was a strong, wonderful, matriarchal household," Baca says.

2. Her family was puzzled when they saw the abstract work Baca had done. "When I showed her my work, my grandmother said to me, 'What is this?' "

3. They incorporated a style of expression that was familiar to the kids—graffiti—with stories about the neighborhood, all turned into art.

4. "My idea was that what we had learned with the <u>interracial</u> work in Los Angeles could be applied to an international scope, from the neighborhood to the global," she says.

5. "If we cannot imagine peace as an active <u>concept</u>, how can we ever hope for it to happen?"

RECALLING DETAILS

1. What was Baca's response to being thrown into an English-speaking classroom?

2. Why were Baca's college years a time of conflict?

3. Why did Baca change styles from abstract to more realistic art?

4. Why were the officials of the city of Los Angeles pleased with Baca's results?

5. Describe Baca's mural *World Wall*.

UNDERSTANDING INFERENCES

In your notebook, write two or three sentences from the biography that support each of the following inferences.

1. The murals Baca and her teenage artists painted helped create a new spirit in the neighborhoods where they appeared.

2. When Baca was young, educators felt that immigrants should shed their first language and culture.

3. Baca's culture has influenced her artistic development.

4. Baca's murals were valuable to the communities in which they were painted.

5. Judith Baca uses murals to try to create unity in the world.

INTERPRETING WHAT YOU HAVE READ

1. How did Judith Baca convince the teenagers to trust her?

2. How do you think graffiti is different from the murals the teenagers made? How is it similar?

3. When people create murals they have to work together. How does this affect the work that is created?

4. Why do you think Baca included teenagers from different gangs in her mural project?

5. What do you think the teenagers who worked on the murals learned from the experience?

ANALYZING QUOTATIONS

Read the following quotation from the biography and answer the questions below.

> "My idea was that what we had learned with the interracial work in Los Angeles could be applied to an international scope, from the neighborhood to the global," she says.

1. What does it mean to move "from the neighborhood to the global"?

2. What do you think this quotation says about Judith Baca?

3. Do you think Baca is being too ambitious? Why or why not?

THINKING CRITICALLY

1. When Baca was young, she says, people thought it was a good thing for all separate ethnic groups to disappear and blend in. Explain why you agree or disagree with this idea.

2. Why do you think Baca's work in Los Angeles gave her the idea of taking her work to the world?

3. How might imagining peace lead to achieving it?

4. What do you think the results of Baca's international work might be?

5. Baca is doing her *World Wall* project to try to create peace. What message would you send on a mural around the world?

GLORIA ESTEFAN

Gloria Estefan performs at the American Music Awards in Los Angeles in 1991, her first stage performance after breaking her back in an accident in 1990. Estefan has combined her Cuban and American heritages to build a successful career in music.

There was an explosion as the truck crashed into the bus. Singer Gloria Estefan (es-TEF-ahn) remembers seeing the front of the bus cave in. Suddenly she was on her back on the floor in unbearable pain. Snow was gently falling into what remained of the bus. "Baby, are you all right?" cried her frantic husband, Emilio Estefan. "I think I broke my back," she said calmly.

It's happened, Estefan remembers thinking. The thing I always feared most. Since her childhood, when she watched her strong father become disabled, having something similar happen to her had been her greatest fear. "I couldn't help it—my eyes filled with tears," she recalls. The ambulance took two hours to reach her. She was given no medicine for the terrible pain because the paramedics wanted her to see a doctor first. They carried her out "through the hole that used to be the windshield," Estefan remembers. "I could feel the snow on my face and see people looking down at me with fear in their faces."

At the hospital, she was given a grim choice. She could be put into a body cast and probably not fully recover. Or she could choose surgery, with its risk of permanent paralysis.[1] Even if the operation was successful, her doctors told the Cuban-born star, she probably would never dance again.

Estefan chose surgery. Four thousand flower bouquets and 48,000 cards arrived from her friends and admirers. Then-President Bush called. But it was after the operation was over that the hard work began. "Being home was difficult. I couldn't do anything for myself," she says. "Some days it seemed I was just trudging along and I would never be able to do anything again."

But Estefan tackled this new challenge the way she has done everything in her life. Her doctors doubted that she would fully

---

1. **paralysis** (puh-RA-luh-suhs) *n.* the state of not being able to move

recover, but Estefan decided they were wrong. She spent long hours exercising and more hours in therapy. "I'm a couch potato, but I've also always known you have to work really hard to get what you want. I had to talk myself into exercising every day. Some days you just want to lie there. But having your health back and being able to do what you want to do are great incentives."[2]

One year later, in 1991, Estefan was on the stage of the American Music Awards. "Before I went out, I was so nervous, my knees were literally[3] knocking," she says. "All I could think was oh my gosh, people are going to think I can't walk."

She proved them wrong, prancing onto the stage and then singing her heart out in what was to become another hit song, "Coming out of the Dark." The song had a special meaning for Estefan. Days after the accident, when she was being flown from one hospital to another, her husband looked out of the helicopter window and saw light breaking through the clouds. Months later when he told her the story, she wrote a song based on what had happened that day.

Songs have always been an important part of Estefan's life. "Since I was three years old, I sang. I sang everything," Estefan says. Cubans, she adds, are "a musical people. We're very passionate about everything—music being one of them." (See **Did You Know?** on page 77 for more information about Cuban music.)

Gloria Fajardo (fah-HAHR-doh) was born in Cuba in 1958, just before Fidel Castro seized power in a revolution. Her father, Manuel Fajardo, was a Cuban soldier. He had been a bodyguard for Cuba's previous president, Fulgencio Batista (fool-GHEN-see-oh bah-TEES-tah). After Castro overthrew Batista, Estefan's family, and many other Cubans who had supported Batista, feared for their safety. They quickly left the island.

In the United States, Estefan's father joined the Central

---

2. **incentives** (ihn-SEHN-tihvz) *n. pl.* encouragements; motivations
3. **literally** (LIH-tuh-ruh-lee) *adv.* actually

Intelligence Agency (CIA). Then he joined the U.S. Army. Gloria and her mother were on their own in Miami, a place that was, at the time, hostile to Cuban immigrants. "My mother was looking for an apartment to live in, and I was a baby. There were signs that said 'No children, no pets, no Cubans.' It was very tough."

Estefan was just learning English as she entered school. In her first-grade class, she was the only Latino student. Her response was to become fanatic[4] about learning English. Six months after entering school, she won an award for reading—in English. To this day, she speaks only the simple Spanish she knew as a child. In an effort to make sure that Estefan knew English, her high school forbade her to take Spanish classes.

Music remained an important part of Estefan's life. She sang along to songs in Spanish and English. She also took guitar lessons, although the lessons "turned me off, because music is like a language to me," she says. The lessons were "tedious, and I wished I could just sit down and play." Soon, however, she knew enough to accompany herself on the guitar.

Estefan's father was sent to Vietnam and returned when Gloria was 10. Soon, people began wondering what was wrong. He forgot simple things. "He'd fall for no reason," Estefan says. Before long, the doctors had an answer. He had multiple sclerosis, a disease that affects the brain. Soon he was unable to care for himself. Estefan's mother, who had been a teacher in Cuba, went back to school to become certified in the United States and began teaching. Estefan began caring for both her father and her younger sister, Becky.

Estefan still made the honor roll in school, but her life was lonely. "I looked so much older than I do now because I was carrying the weight of the whole world on my shoulders. I was used to being so full of responsibility, never being able to let go because I was afraid to. It was a situation that I could see no way of getting out of."

---

4. **fanatic** (fuh-NAT-ihk) *adj.* obsessed; too enthusiastic

In high school, Estefan was chubby and shy and thought of herself as a loner. "When my father was ill, music was my escape. I would lock myself up in my room for hours and just sing. I wouldn't cry—I refused to cry. Music was the only way I had to let go."

In 1975, Gloria met Emilio Estefan when he came to her high school to speak about being a band leader. He later talked to Estefan and several of her friends who wanted advice on putting together their own group. She also sang for him. She saw Estefan again at a wedding, where he asked her to sing several songs with his band, the Miami Latin Boys. The band was angry at Estefan. Why was he asking this untrained, probably untalented, kid to sing with them? Emilio Estefan told them not to worry.

The band was wowed by Gloria's voice. Soon after, Emilio Estefan asked her to join the group. She told him she was too busy with school. She had just entered the University of Miami, and she wanted to focus on studying.

He called again and told her it would be "like a hobby." This was the beginning of the Miami Sound Machine. Estefan kept studying, but "All of a sudden I was going to parties every weekend, singing with a whole band behind me, making money for it, and enjoying every second."

Within a few months, the Miami Sound Machine was the top band in Miami. Estefan began to remake herself. She lost weight, began a strict exercise program, and became the slim, outgoing singer her fans now admire. With experience, she became more comfortable in front of the band. "I loved [performing] more and more and little by little it just started coming out more," she says. "I was very shy, and it was a painful process for me."

In 1978, she and Estefan married. Two years later, their son Nayib was born. Although Gloria had graduated from college, she gave up her idea of becoming a psychologist and decided to concentrate on music. By 1982, she was the center of the group.

At first the Miami Sound Machine was known only in the Spanish community in Miami. Then they signed with CBS Records' Latin music division and became wildly popular in

Central and South America. In 1984, their song written in English, "Dr. Beat," caused a sensation on English-speaking radio stations in the United States. Discos CBS International, the record label's Latin division, had promoted the Miami Sound Machine as a Latin American group. They didn't know what to do with the band's success in the English-speaking market, so they finally agreed to switch the band to CBS's Epic Records. The group's 1985 album, *Primitive Love,* was a smash hit. The single "Conga," from that album, was the first to appear on *Billboard* magazine's dance, pop, Latin, and black charts at the same time. Estefan and her group became stars.

Since then, the group has sold millions of albums. Emilio Estefan's management of the group has earned him and his wife an estimated worth of $28 million. She is considered the country's most successful Latina entertainer. Estefan has done more than just sing, though. In 1992, when Hurricane Andrew tore a path through Miami, she needed only two weeks to organize an all-star concert that raised $2 million for the hurricane's victims. "We needed a party after all that tragedy," she says.

In 1993, Estefan released *Mi Tierra (My Homeland).* "It is, like all my pop music, reflective of my cultural mix of Cuban American. But this is really a tribute to my homeland, one side of my roots," she says. "It's my favorite project I've ever done." Part of the reason for the record is to "do something international that would open doors for a lot of Latin musicians and help younger Cubans become more aware of their musical roots," she says. The recording won a Grammy award in 1994.

Over the years, Estefan has remained true to her heritage. "The one thing that I think has really carried us through the years is that you have to stay true to the music you really love to do. And there will always be people who will tell you, 'That won't work.' You've got to persevere.[5] Stick with it—that's the main thing."

---

5. **persevere** (puhr-suh-VIHR) *v.* to keep at something regardless of opposition or discouragement

Did You Know? Although Cuban music takes many forms, perhaps the best known is salsa. This fast-paced dance music, which is based on Latin American dance forms, such as the rhumba, became popular in the United States in the 1960s and 1970s when Cubans and immigrants from other Latin American countries came to the United States in large numbers. The best-known salsa artists are Cuban performer Celia Cruz and Puerto Rican performer Tito Puente. The Miami Latin Boys, the group that changed its name to the Miami Sound Machine, made its reputation with salsa. Since then, the Miami Sound Machine has created a new sound that blends salsa, ballads, and U.S. pop.

AFTER YOU READ

EXPLORING YOUR RESPONSES

1. Gloria Estefan was given the choice between a dangerous operation and another, less dangerous treatment that would not allow her to fully recover. How could a person make such a decision?

2. Estefan says that you have to work hard for what you want. Describe a time that you, or someone you know, worked hard to achieve a goal.

3. Which part of Estefan's life do you think has been the most difficult? Explain.

4. Estefan says that when she was young, music was her escape. How can music help a person "escape"?

5. If you were a professional musician, what kind of music would you most like to play? Why?

UNDERSTANDING WORDS IN CONTEXT

Read the following sentences from the biography. Think about what each underlined word means. In your notebook, write what the word means as it is used in the sentence.

1. She could be put into a body cast and probably not fully recover. Or she could choose surgery, with its risk of permanent paralysis. Even if the operation was successful, her doctors told the Cuban-born star, she probably would never dance again.

2. "Some days you just want to lie there. But having your health back and being able to do what you want to do are great incentives."

3. "Before I went out, I was so nervous, my knees were literally knocking," she says.

4. Her response was to become <u>fanatic</u> about learning English. Six months after entering school, she won an award for reading—in English.

5. "You've got to <u>persevere</u>. Stick with it—that's the main thing."

RECALLING DETAILS

1. Why was Estefan so afraid of becoming disabled?

2. What is the history of the song "Coming out of the Dark"?

3. Why did Estefan's family leave Cuba?

4. Describe Estefan's growth as a performer.

5. Why is *Mi Tierra* Estefan's favorite project?

UNDERSTANDING INFERENCES

In your notebook, write two or three sentences that support each of the following inferences.

1. Estefan's response to difficult situations is to work harder.

2. Estefan was forced to grow up quickly.

3. Estefan has a strong drive to improve herself.

4. Gloria Estefan feels a strong tie to Cuba.

5. Estefan feels a need to give back to her people and her community.

INTERPRETING WHAT YOU HAVE READ

1. How did lessons that Estefan learned early in her life help her recover from her accident?

2. Estefan says that Cubans are passionate. What do you think she is passionate about? Explain.

3. Why do you think that Estefan began to remake herself when she joined the Miami Sound Machine?

4. What can you tell about Estefan's music from the success of "Conga"?

5. Why do you think that Estefan waited until 1993 to record *Mi Tierra?*

ANALYZING QUOTATIONS

Read the following quotation from the biography and answer the questions below.

> *"The one thing that I think has really carried us through the years is that you have to stay true to the music you really love to do. And there will always be people who will tell you, 'That won't work.' You've got to persevere. Stick with it—that's the main thing."*

1. How can a person "stay true to the music" he or she loves?

2. Give two examples of how Gloria Estefan persevered in her life.

3. Do you agree that persevering is "the main thing"? Explain.

THINKING CRITICALLY

1. What do you think Estefan learned from caring for her sister and her father when she was a teenager?

2. How can music help a person "let go"?

3. If Estefan becomes a psychologist, as she originally planned, what do you think she has learned from her singing career that might help her in her work?

4. If you were going to make up a slogan that captured what has made Gloria Estefan successful, what would it be?

5. Estefan organized a concert to raise money for victims of Hurricane Andrew. What cause would you most like to help? What would you do?

EDWARD JAMES OLMOS

Mexican American actor Edward James Olmos confers with Jaime Escalante on the set of "Futures," a TV program designed to interest students in mathematics. Olmos portrayed Escalante in the movie *Stand and Deliver*.

A terrified country watched as Los Angeles exploded in riots in 1992 after motorist Rodney King was beaten by police officers. Actor Edward James Olmos was heading for an interview at a local TV station. He was planning to plead with people to go back to their homes instead of rioting. Suddenly, in front of him, a young boy was shot. "By the time we got out and tried to help him, it was pretty late," Olmos says. One of the boy's friends came up to Olmos. "What are you going to do now, actor boy? This is real life, actor boy."

Shaken, Olmos continued driving to the TV station. "I was so angry and so frustrated that I ended up just declaring on the station that I was going to go out and start sweeping the streets," the actor says. "I just said I was going to do it. And that I was going to start at the first A.M.E. Church over on Adams."

When Olmos got there, a truckload of children pulled up to sweep the streets. "We started to walk down the street, and pretty soon there were people coming out of their homes starting to sweep and clean. Children started to run around and pick up paper and trash. By the time 20 minutes had gone by, we were 40 strong."

By the end of the day, there were 600 people helping Olmos. "The second day, there were over 10,000," Olmos says. "There was no organization. Everybody made the choice themselves to be there."

For Olmos, the experience showed him something he had known all along. "Whenever you give from a feeling inside, you receive back a tremendous sense of self-esteem and self-worth, which is something you can't buy," he says. "You can only get it from giving."

Olmos was born in 1947 in East Los Angeles. His father had a sixth-grade education when he immigrated to the United States from Mexico. He returned to high school and graduated here. His mother, a Mexican American, had graduated from the eighth grade. She went back to school after her children were grown and graduated from junior college in 1989.

When Olmos was eight, his parents divorced. He and his brothers and sisters grew up in Boyle Heights in Los Angeles, where it seemed everyone was an immigrant. Latinos lived next to Korean and Chinese people. "Inside this world, everyone was the same," Olmos recalls. "We were all poor. And the only way to survive it was through a constant struggle of trying to be better today than you were yesterday. So that's what I tried to do—first with baseball, then with music and drama."

There was little respect for the immigrants' languages and cultures when Olmos went to school. "When I got to Belvedere Elementary, there was a sign on the wall that said, 'If it isn't worth saying in English, it isn't worth saying at all,' " Olmos says.

In striving to better himself, Olmos took up baseball with a passion. He won the California batting championship. When he was 14 years old, he was practicing with major leaguers in the California winter league. "Baseball was the biggest character building influence of my youth," he says. "It taught me self-discipline, determination,[1] perseverance, and patience—all of which have been key ingredients to what I have done since."

When he was 15, Olmos turned his passion to a new field—music. "It's hard to explain this sudden change of heart," he says. "I think I felt that music could offer me bigger dreams. I wanted to sing and dance, but I really couldn't sing. I was the worst. However, I worked at it, like I had with baseball, until I developed a kind of style. I also taught myself to play the piano. And I'd already learned to dance from my father."

Olmos started a band. By the mid-1960s, it was playing regularly at nightclubs. But even while he was playing music, Olmos never forgot the value his parents placed on education. If they cared enough about it to go back to school as adults, he could make it a priority, too. During the day, Olmos went to college at East Los Angeles City College. Nights belonged to his work with the band.

---

1. **determination** (dih-tehr-muh-NAY-shuhn) *n.* a firm intention; persistence

Olmos thought that acting would improve his stage presence as a singer with the band. Then he discovered that he preferred acting to music. He broke up the band and kept the van. Then he began a furniture delivery business that could support his acting—and his family. He had met and married Kaija Keel, and they had two sons.

For years, Olmos was a struggling actor in Los Angeles. He worked in small theaters, then in larger theaters. In the early 1970s, he began to get bit parts on television shows like "Hawaii Five-O" and "Kojak."

In the acting business, hard work can sometimes lead to a lucky break. For Olmos, that happened in 1978 when he won the part of El Pachuco, a flashy, strutting Mexican American in the play *Zoot Suit*. "I spoke in caló, street jive from the streets of L.A.—a mix of Spanish, English, and gypsy," Olmos says. "They asked me if I could dance, and I hit a perfect set of splits, turning the brim of my hat as I came up."

The play was a musical drama set in Los Angeles and based on the Sleepy Lagoon case. (See **Did You Know?** on page 87 for more information about this case.) *Zoot Suit* became the talk of the town. For the first time, a big-time play was tackling the issues of the city's Latino population. Olmos felt "a tremendous responsibility" in the part. "I was bringing to life the first real Latin character and Latin culture seen on the American stage."

Olmos wowed Los Angeles. Although the show was only supposed to run ten weeks, it ran more than a year before it moved to Broadway. There, Olmos was nominated for Broadway's highest honor, a Tony award.

After that, things got a little easier. Olmos starred in the movie version of the play, and then in other movies, such as *Wolfen* and *Blade Runner.* He was offered a major role in the violent film *Scarface,* about a Cuban immigrant who becomes a drug dealer. Olmos refused. "They offered me hundreds of thousands of dollars," he remembers. "I just couldn't find myself inside that movie." The violence and stereotypical behavior didn't fit Olmos's ideas of the parts he wanted to play.

When he was offered the title role in *The Ballad of Gregorio Cortez,* though, Olmos jumped at the chance. The movie was made for TV, and Olmos thought it had an important message. "The film portrayed one of the first legendary heroes of Latin ancestry ever shown on the screen." Cortez was a young Mexican who was unjustly charged with murder because of prejudice. He avoided a 600-man posse for nearly two weeks before being captured. After the film was completed, Olmos tried for more than five years to get the film shown in movie theaters. No one wanted it, so he started showing it every Saturday, for free, in a Hollywood theater. He turned down about a half-million dollars in acting work to promote the movie. Olmos finally succeeded, and the film was shown across the country.

What made Olmos a household name was becoming Lieutenant Martin Castillo in the 1980s TV hit "Miami Vice." At the time he was offered it, "We didn't have any money," Olmos says. "We weren't starving on the streets. We just didn't have any money." But at first, Olmos refused the role on "Miami Vice," too. Olmos wouldn't take the job because the producer wanted an exclusive.[2] That meant that Olmos would not be allowed to work on anything else. That wasn't acceptable to him.

The producer called back and offered more money. Olmos said no. He called again. "On the fourth call, he raised the price again, and I said to myself, 'Now he's offering more money for eight weeks' work than my father probably made in his lifetime.'" But he still said no. On the fifth call, Olmos was offered the job—with a nonexclusive contract. "No one in the history of television has ever had such a contract. Producers do not sign contracts like that."

Olmos had problems with some of the one-dimensional[3] stories of "Miami Vice" and with some of its views toward

2. **exclusive** (ihks-KLOO-sihv) *n.* a contract that limits someone to work only for one person or group
3. **one-dimensional** (WUHN duh-MEHN-shuhn-uhl) *adj.* lacking depth; too simple

women. Olmos complained at the time, "Women are just used as decor.[4] Once in a while, we'll have a story in which a woman is shown in a positive light, but mainly, they're suffering victims."

It was not until the movie *Stand and Deliver* that Olmos found another story about Latinos that he felt was worth telling. This was the story of Jaime Escalante (es-kah-LAHN-teh), a Latino math teacher in East Los Angeles whose hard work and encouragement of Latino kids in East L.A. led to remarkable success. (See the biography of Jaime Escalante on page 118.)

Olmos feels that involving Latinos in the arts is extremely important. "I think the non–Hispanic culture will be facing a critical time, unless it understands, first of all, that the Latin American is in the majority in the Americas, not the minority," he says. "It's essential that the arts open up to the Hispanic culture. *Stand and Deliver* was a surprise to a lot of people, whereas to us, it was simply a confirmation[5] of our own beliefs."

To play Escalante, Olmos spent hundreds of hours watching him. He tape-recorded him talking and spent hours trying to copy Escalante's speech. He also gained 40 pounds to play the role. Olmos won an Academy Award nomination for Best Actor for his portrayal.

Olmos has since directed and starred in *American Me,* a warning tale about what happens to a teenage drug lord when he ends up in prison. Olmos wants to help young people understand that they can make it out of poor backgrounds, just as he did. He spends hundreds of hours every year visiting high schools and tells students, "Listen, I'm your worst nightmare. With me, all your excuses go out the window. You can't use any of them to excuse why you can't cope or achieve your full potential. You're looking at a guy with an upbringing no different from any one of yours. I'm just the average guy who learned to hit the home run."

---

4. **decor** (day-KOHR) *n.* decoration; the decorative scheme of a room
5. **confirmation** (kahn-fuhr-MAY-shuhn) *n.* proof; evidence

What Olmos did was to focus on what he wanted, work until he got it, and never compromise[6] his principles. It is that honesty and hard work that audiences understand, and that shines through his acting and his life.

> **Did You Know?** *The play* Zoot Suit *is based on the true story of the Sleepy Lagoon case in Los Angeles. One August day in 1942, the body of a Mexican American was found near the Sleepy Lagoon swimming hole. The police response was to crack down on Mexican American street gangs and arrest 300 young Mexican Americans. Seventeen of these young people were later tried for the murder and convicted of everything from murder to assault, even though there were no witnesses. When a higher court reversed the convictions, one result was a wave of anti-Mexican sentiment that led to the Zoot Suit riots in 1943, in which many young Mexican Americans were attacked.*

6. **compromise** (KAHM-pruh-meyez) *v.* give away something to gain something in return

AFTER YOU READ

EXPLORING YOUR RESPONSES

1. When Olmos saw the boy shot during the riot, his reaction was to clean up the streets. What might you have done?

2. Olmos survived his childhood by trying to be better each day than he was the day before. How might this attitude help someone survive poor circumstances?

3. Baseball taught Olmos about building character when he was young. What other activities can build character? Explain.

4. Olmos had a "lucky break" when he won the part of El Pachuco. Do you believe in lucky breaks? Why or why not?

5. Olmos turned down the starring role in *Scarface*. Would you have done the same thing? Why or why not?

UNDERSTANDING WORDS IN CONTEXT

Read the following sentences from the biography. Think about what each underlined word means. In your notebook, write what the word means as it is used in the sentence.

1. "Baseball was the biggest character-building influence of my youth," he says. "It taught me self-discipline, determination, perseverance, and patience—all of which have been key ingredients to what I have done since."

2. Olmos had problems with some of the one-dimensional stories of "Miami Vice" and with some of its views toward women.

3. "Women are just used as decor. Once in a while, we'll have a story in which a woman is shown in a positive light, but mainly, they're suffering victims."

4. "*Stand and Deliver* was a surprise to a lot of people, whereas to us, it was simply a confirmation of our own beliefs."

5. What Olmos did was to focus on what he wanted, work until he got it, and never <u>compromise</u> his principles.

RECALLING DETAILS

1. Describe Olmos's early life.

2. What qualities helped Olmos become a good baseball player, singer, and dancer?

3. How did Olmos's parents teach him that education was important?

4. What was Olmos's lucky break in acting?

5. Why is Olmos so eager to speak at high schools?

UNDERSTANDING INFERENCES

In your notebook, write two or three sentences from the biography that support each of the following inferences.

1. Olmos has a talent for helping people see different viewpoints.

2. Olmos was willing to sacrifice to become an actor.

3. When Olmos wants something, he works hard to achieve it.

4. Olmos thinks that other cultures in the United States have a lot to learn from Latinos.

5. Olmos thinks actors should believe in the roles they play.

INTERPRETING WHAT YOU HAVE READ

1. Why do you think so many people joined Olmos on the streets to clean up after the Los Angeles riots?

2. At Olmos's elementary school, a sign said "If it isn't worth saying in English, it isn't worth saying at all." Why do you think people believed this?

3. Olmos said that baseball taught him "self-discipline, determination, perseverance, and patience." How could playing baseball teach him these things?

4. Why do you think Olmos turned down the role in *Scarface,* a violent movie, but went out of his way to direct and star in *American Me,* another violent movie?

5. Why do you think having a nonexclusive contract with "Miami Vice" was so important to Olmos?

ANALYZING QUOTATIONS

Read the following quotation from the biography and answer the questions below.

> "Stand and Deliver *was a surprise to a lot of people, whereas to us, it was simply a confirmation of our own beliefs.*"

1. Why does Olmos think that *Stand and Deliver* was a surprise to a lot of people?

2. Which of Olmos's beliefs do you think *Stand and Deliver* confirms?

3. How could a movie "confirm people's beliefs"?

CRITICAL THINKING

1. In Olmos's elementary school, people were allowed to speak only English. Do you agree or disagree with this policy?

2. How do you think Olmos's life might have been different if he had grown up wealthy? Explain your answer.

3. Olmos says, "It's essential that the arts open up to the Hispanic culture." Explain why you agree or disagree with this statement.

4. Which of Olmos's actions do you admire most? Explain your answer.

5. Olmos tells high school students that he throws all of their excuses "out the window." Do you agree with him? Explain.

FERNANDO BUJONES

Fernando Bujones was the first male U.S. dancer to win a gold medal in the Varna Competition in Bulgaria, an important international contest for ballet dancers. Bujones now also choreographs, using his Cuban heritage to expand his work.

Fernando Bujones (boo-HOH-nes) set the ballet world talking in the early 1970s. He was a brash,[1] talented newcomer who wowed audiences with his grace and technique. He also was not shy about his ability. "I know very well just how good I am," he said in an interview at the time. "I know what I can do, and it's a very exhilarating[2] feeling . . . so I just let myself go." That confidence was at the heart of his stunning performing ability. It also earned him a reputation as the "bad boy" of ballet.

When Bujones started his ballet training, becoming a celebrated ballet star was the last thing on his mind. He was born in Miami in 1955. The next year, when Bujones was 8 years old, his parents returned to their native Cuba. "I just wouldn't eat," Bujones says. "I was impossible. My mother was getting desperate, and she thought that some kind of exercise would stimulate my appetite." Because his mother was an actress and knew Alicia Alonso's famous dance company, she enrolled him in a ballet class at Alonso's school. (See ***Did You Know?*** on page 95 for more information about this famous Cuban ballerina.)

"At first, I saw it as a fun thing. I saw the other boys jumping around, and it was like a game. I enjoyed it," Bujones says. When he was 10, his parents divorced, and Bujones and his mother returned to Miami. For a year, he took no lessons. Then he was persuaded to play the role of the child prince in the ballet *The Nutcracker.* Before long, Bujones had returned to studying ballet.

His mother, Mary Bujones, was working as a stage manager for a ballet company in Miami in 1967 when Jacques d'Amboise of the New York City Ballet came to Miami as a guest artist. The New York City Ballet is one of the premier[3] ballet companies in

---

1. **brash** (BRASH) *adj.* reckless; impulsive
2. **exhilarating** (ihg-ZIHL-uh-rayt-ihng) *adj.* exciting
3. **premier** (prih-MYEER) *adj.* most important; best

the country. Mary arranged an audition for her 12-year-old son. D'Amboise was impressed enough to offer the youngster a summer scholarship to the School of American Ballet (SAB). It was a big vote of confidence. SAB has trained some of the finest dancers in the United States. That summer, Bujones and his mother traveled to New York City. The next fall, Bujones was offered a full-time scholarship.

"Well, that was something to think about!" Bujones remembers. "It was a big decision we had to make. Finally, of course, we decided to move to New York. We all piled into a Volkswagen—my mother, my cousin, myself, and my dog—and we drove all the way from Miami to New York."

From then on, Bujones gave up the life of a teenager for the life of a dancer. "The first year, I worked hard, but it wasn't until the second year that I looked inside myself and realized my own talent." This concentration and determination led to his winning roles in one student performance after another. At the age of 14, he was asked to join the New York City Ballet.

Bujones turned down the offer because he loved the more traditional ballet of other companies. Instead, he put his energy into working still harder. "I don't resent having been like that when I was younger, because that's what made me accomplish the technique that I have today, which can only happen when you are extremely concentrated." In addition to his classes, Bujones studied with his cousin Zeida Méndez, who came to New York with him and his mother in 1967. "It hurt," Bujones says of the hours of extra work he did with his cousin, "and that kind of work where we persisted[4] even beyond hurting is what has made me the stamina[5] dancer that I am." When he graduated from the school at age 17, he had several offers from national ballet companies.

Bujones chose American Ballet Theatre, which specializes in the ballet he likes best—the classics from the 1800s. They were

---

4. **persisted** (puhr-SIHST-uhd) *v.* continued; stayed with it
5. **stamina** (STAM-uh-nuh) *adj.* having staying power; enduring

the dances he had studied in Cuba. Within months, Bujones, the prodigy,[6] was dancing principal[7] roles. In 1974, when he was 19, Bujones decided to compete in the Varna Competition in Bulgaria, an international contest for ballet dancers. No American had ever won the gold medal, but that didn't stop Bujones. "It's in my nature, in my blood, to be adventurous." The gamble paid off. "I remember waiting anxiously for the judges' decision," he says. "Of course, no one told you anything. My mother was the first to give me the news." Bujones had become the first male U.S. dancer to win the gold medal.

The dancer returned to the United States in triumph, only to find that another event had captured the attention of the ballet world. Mikhail Baryshnikov (bah-RIHSH-nuh-kawv) had just defected[8] from the Soviet Union to the United States. The Russian dancer immediately became the star of the U.S. dance world.

Bujones felt he had been robbed of the spotlight. When asked for a comment on Baryshnikov, he told a reporter, "Baryshnikov has the publicity, but I have the talent." Both were stars at ABT and their relationship was uneasy for years.

During this time, Bujones remained close to his family. He lived with his mother and cousin in New York until he met and married Maria Kubitschek, daughter of Brazil's former president. They had a child, Alejandra. Ballet watchers said that the change mellowed the star. Bujones seems to agree. "Before, I spent so much of life in classes, rehearsals, and performances, and I was terribly insulated.[9] Though my family . . . was always trying to open my mind, with great culture behind it, it was still a closed sort of [life]."

In 1984, Bujones began to expand his work by choreographing[10] dances. He wanted, he said, to design a dance that would highlight "my Spanish tradition."

---

6. **prodigy** (PRAHD-uh-jee) *n.* a highly talented child
7. **principal** (PRIHN-suh-puhl) *adj.* leading
8. **defected** (dih-FEHKT-uhd) *v.* abandoned one country to live in another
9. **insulated** (IHN-suh-layt-uhd) *v.* kept unaware; shielded
10. **choreographing** (KAWR-ee-uh-graf-ihng) *v.* designing dances

The next year, Baryshnikov was named the artistic director of ABT. In 1985, after a major disagreement with Baryshnikov, Bujones resigned from the only ballet home he had ever known. He became a guest artist, dancing around the world with different ballet companies. Then the Boston Ballet offered him a role as principal dancer, with the understanding that he would be able to guest star elsewhere. In 1994, he became the artistic director of Ballet Mississippi. In the 1994-95 season he will be the artistic director at the Bay Ballet Theatre in Tampa, Florida. Becoming artistic director is the natural next step for a dancer who has the desire to make his mark on his profession. Bujones remains a celebrated dancer, with the fire and drive that led him to be widely considered the United States's best native-born ballet dancer.

"Greatness depends on taking risks," Bujones says, "and my dancing must always be taking chances. I enjoy making it difficult for myself. I enjoy taking risks because it's part of my personality and part of what my dancing is. It's part of what I've been criticized for, which I hope one day people will understand."

> **Did You Know?** Alicia Alonso was one of the best-known ballerinas in the world when she decided, after the revolution in Cuba in 1959, to return to her native country. Her reputation and the quality of the ballet school and national company she established in Cuba have made both organizations landmarks in international dance circles.

AFTER YOU READ

EXPLORING YOUR RESPONSES

1. How can having as much confidence as Bujones has help a person? How can it hurt?

2. What would you like to study that would be worth making the sacrifices Bujones made? Explain.

3. Bujones felt he was unappreciated once Baryshnikov defected to the United States. What are some ways people can deal with this feeling?

4. Bujones gave up the life of a teenager to devote himself to dance. How do you think that might have affected him?

5. Do you agree with Bujones that one must take risks to be great ? Explain your answer.

UNDERSTANDING WORDS IN CONTEXT

Read the following sentences from the biography. Think about what each underlined word means. In your notebook, write what the word means as it is used in the sentence.

1. He was a brash, talented newcomer who wowed audiences with his grace and technique. He was also not shy about his ability.

2. "I know what I can do, and it's a very exhilarating feeling . . . so I just let myself go."

3. The New York City Ballet is one of the premier ballet companies in the country.

4. "It hurt," Bujones says of the hours of extra work with his cousin, "and that kind of work where we persisted even beyond hurting is what has made me the stamina dancer that I am."

5. "Before, I spent so much of life in classes, rehearsals, and performances, and I was terribly underlined{insulated}."

RECALLING DETAILS

1. Why did Bujones first study ballet?
2. What helped the young dancer to become the master he is today?
3. Why did Bujones decide to join the American Ballet Theatre?
4. Why did Bujones get less attention than he wished after he won the gold medal at Varna?
5. What else has Bujones done in his career besides dance?

UNDERSTANDING INFERENCES

In your notebook, write two or three sentences from the biography that support each of the following inferences.

1. Bujones's mother was right to think he showed unusual promise as a ballet dancer.
2. Bujones's family made changes in their lives to help him become a great dancer.
3. Concentrating on dancing helps dancers develop their talent.
4. Having a wife and child caused Bujones to expand his world.
5. Bujones is respected as more than just a dancer.

INTERPRETING WHAT YOU HAVE READ

1. How did Bujones's mother help his development as a dancer?
2. What do you think it meant to Bujones when he said, "I looked inside myself and realized my own talent"?
3. Bujones refers to professional ballet as a "closed kind of life." Do you think this might be true? Why?
4. Why do you think competing in the Varna Competition was considered adventurous?

5. What did you learn about the ballet world from reading this biography?

ANALYZING QUOTATIONS

Read the following quotation from the biography and answer the questions below.

> *"I know very well just how good I am," he said in an interview at the time. "I know what I can do, and it's a very exhilarating feeling . . . so I just let myself go."*

1. What do you think Bujones means when he says, "I just let myself go"?

2. Do you think this kind of attitude is necessary for someone to be a star? Explain your answer.

3. How can people judge how good they are?

THINKING CRITICALLY

1. What do you think early success did to Bujones?

2. How might being insulated help a person's career? How might it hurt a career?

3. How do you think the changes in Bujones's personal life have affected his career?

4. Why might people criticize someone who takes risks?

5. Do you think success depends on taking risks? Why or why not?

MIRIAM COLÓN

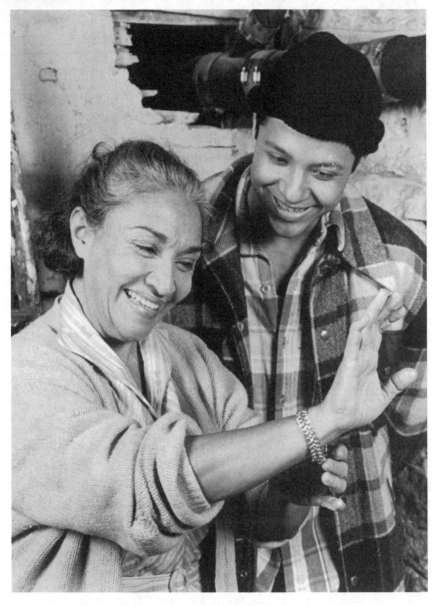

Miriam Colón and Joe Quintero in "The Boiler Room," which was presented in English and Spanish by Colón's company, The Puerto Rican Traveling Theatre. This troupe reaches out to the Latino community in New York City by bringing theater to the city's neighborhoods.

It was a steaming summer day in New York City in 1967. Two Puerto Rican teenagers were walking by the park when they saw a crowd. Intrigued,[1] they walked closer. They watched as actors spoke passionately to one another. What was this? It was a play about a family from Puerto Rico who had moved to the Bronx. "This is about me," one teenager thought. "This is about my life."

That was the response Miriam Colón hoped for when she founded the Puerto Rican Traveling Theatre in 1967. "The streets are a phenomenal[2] place to play and reach audiences," she says. "At the beginning, we just wanted to share what we had with as many people as possible."

The first play the group performed was *The Ox Cart* by the Puerto Rican playwright René Marqués (mahr-KEHZ). (See **Did You Know?** on page 104 for more information about Marqués.) "When I saw how the audiences reacted to this play about a Puerto Rican family—black kids crying, Jewish ladies saying, 'That's MY family, too'—I realized all you need is a good play. It doesn't matter who wrote it, as long as it's relevant,"[3] Colón says.

"I didn't have in mind to create something called the Puerto Rican Traveling Theatre," Colón recalls. She had decided to produce *The Ox Cart* "because it spoke about a reality. It was a wonderful play that brought, as we saw, a wonderful audience reaction. When I brought it to the streets in 1967, people kept asking what we were going to call the company. I decided that since it would be traveling about the city, it should be called the Puerto Rican Traveling Theatre."

Colón was a natural to bring Puerto Rican theater to the

---

1. **intrigued** (ihn-TREEGD) *adj.* caused interest or curiosity
2. **phenomenal** (fih-NAH-muh-nuhl) *adj.* remarkable; extraordinary
3. **relevant** (REH-luh-vuhnt) *adj.* appropriate; related to people's needs

United States. She was born in 1945 in Ponce (POHN-ceh), Puerto Rico, to working-class parents. They moved to San Juan when Colón was 8 years old. When she reached junior high school, theater became the center of her life. She was allowed to sit in on classes at the University of Puerto Rico. When she was still a junior high school student, she was given a role in a play at the university.

Colón's mother told her to follow her dream. "She told me, 'If you want to, be an actor, as long as you don't come home too late.' " And when Colón did stay out late, "her focus was on whether I had eaten and not on stopping me from doing things or being enterprising.[4] She never pushed me away from the direction I wanted to go."

Colón's mother also gave her daughter the time and freedom to do what she wanted. "No one ever stepped in my way. I didn't have a brother tell me it was my responsibility to cook and clean because I was the sister." Colón's mother "has been the major force in my life. To this day, I am very, very attached to her. She is my role model . . . a wonderful, warm woman. I am totally sure of her love—the only thing I'm sure of in my life."

With that encouragement, Colón enrolled at the University of Puerto Rico and joined an acting group. After graduating, she won a scholarship to the Dramatic Workshop and Technical Institute in New York City. Soon she became the first Puerto Rican asked to join the renowned Actor's Studio in New York City.

It wasn't long before *The New York Times* was calling Colón "the most famous Puerto Rican actress in America." She worked on Broadway and in film. Among the many films she made were two with Marlon Brando, *One-Eyed Jacks* and *The Appaloosa*. She has acted in more than 250 TV shows. What has brought Colón her most lasting fame, though, was the founding of the Puerto Rican Traveling Theatre. She had help in achieving this dream from her husband, George Edgar. Edgar was a businessman and a

---

4. **enterprising** (EHN-tuhr-preye-zihng) *adj.* being spirited and independent

theatrical producer whom Colón describes as "a very strong man" who helped the company succeed.

When Colón founded the theater group, she had distinct[5] ideas about her goals. "We wanted bilingual theater. We wanted to be a Puerto Rican group energizing[6] something in the community. We wanted to emphasize[7] Puerto Rican culture," Colón explains. The group's first performances were in English, but they added Spanish performances. "It soon appeared that people wanted us to act in Spanish, too, and that's how it happened." Today, the Spanish and English performances remain. "I want Hispanic youngsters to take pride in the language of their parents and at the same time I want to keep those older people in the habit of listening to spoken Spanish literature."

On other nights when the performances are in English, "you can see an audience, sometimes, of all-Hispanic background. There's a generation that is more comfortable in English."

It may seem easy to memorize the Spanish for a part once you have learned the English, but Colón says this is not true. "Every syllable, every word must be spoken perfectly fluently," she says. "We've had little accidents, laughable ones. Someone might forget which language we're working in and start the show in the wrong language. Someone just coughs and they make it right."

That first summer, and many afterward, the traveling theater performed on the street, in parks, from the back of a flatbed truck. But in 1974, Colón saw an abandoned firehouse in New York City and decided to turn it into a home for the Puerto Rican Traveling Theatre. "Existing from summer to summer was not enough," she says. "We wanted a roof over our heads."

Since its founding, the acting group had been based in Colón's apartment. There was never enough money. But once Colón made up her mind that the firehouse would be the group's home, she worked tirelessly for two years. She met with officials

---

5. **distinct** (dih-STIHNGKT) *adj.* different; separate
6. **energizing** (EH-nuhr-jeyez-ihng) *v.* giving out strength and eagerness
7. **emphasize** (EHM-fuh-seyez) *v.* stress or feature

from the city. She wrote countless letters. Finally, in 1976, Colón won the right to lease the building for $221 a month.

That wasn't enough. Colón began a huge fund-raising campaign to transform[8] the old building into a proper theater. In 1981, the building opened, with a 196-seat theater, rehearsal rooms, a shop to make scenery, and offices. Miriam Colón, almost single-handedly, had led a drive that raised more than $1 million and brought Latino theater into the light in New York City.

In 1976, George Edgar, Colón's husband and partner, died. "I was devastated,"[9] she remembers. She tried to lose herself in her work, "trying to turn the energy out instead of in." Then she met her current husband, who was acting in one of the company's plays. She was still mourning the death of George Edgar. "I really was not looking for romance. I was amazed that I still had the capacity to love and trust and give of myself."

Today the firehouse is not just the home for performances of the Puerto Rican Traveling Theatre. It is also much more. The company's Training Unit accepts talented students who cannot afford acting, music, or dance lessons, and trains them for free. The inspiration came from watching young people become excited about seeing their first live theater. "That's when the idea of a training unit for youngsters became very firm in my mind," Colón says. "There had to be a way we could extend and share what some of us knew." More than 250 students train every year. Fifty of these go on to audition for professional roles.

There is also a Playwrights Unit that helps Latino writers develop their plays. Colón wants these playwrights to examine their culture. "I am deeply interested in urging young writers to explore the unique experience of having Spanish roots but being brought up in America, particularly here in New York," she says. "We give them the opportunity to use our facilities and to develop their works and to make their mistakes in the privacy of their classmates and peers."

---

8. **transform** (tranz-FAWRM) *v.* change
9. **devastated** (DEH-vuh-stayt-uhd) *v.* destroyed; ruined

Besides the productions in the firehouse theater, there is still an annual tour that 10,000 playgoers see each summer in every part of New York City. As it has from the beginning, the tour goes to parks, playgrounds, and prisons. The international tours of the Puerto Rican Traveling Theatre take the company's plays to places as far from New York as Spain, Colombia, and Mexico.

The task of sustaining[10] the Puerto Rican Traveling Theatre may seem impossible at times, but Colón is determined to keep this voice of the Latino community alive.

One of Colón's goals is to change the perception[11] that all Latinos can fit easily into a mold. "In contrast to the stereotypes of Hispanics on television and in films, we in Hispanic theater try to depict[12] people with all their defects and all their virtues," she says. "Audiences appreciate that."

> **Did You Know?** René Marqués is the most famous Puerto Rican playwright of the 20th century. Born in 1919, he became the island's dramatic voice in the 1950s and 1960s with plays that addressed the issue of Puerto Rican cultural identity. His best-known play, The Ox Cart (La Carreta), focuses on the story of a family who moves from the Puerto Rican mountains to a hard life in the United States. Marqués studied drama at Columbia University in New York City and is now a professor at the University of Puerto Rico, Río Piedras. He is also an essayist and novelist.

---

10. **sustaining** (suh-STAYN-ihng) *v.* keeping something going; supporting
11. **perception** (puhr-SEHP-shuhn) *n.* belief; feeling
12. **depict** (dih-PIHKT) *v.* show; represent

AFTER YOU READ

EXPLORING YOUR RESPONSES

1. Miriam Colón's mother gave her the time and freedom to pursue her interests. What else can parents do to encourage their children?

2. Tell about a play or TV show you have seen that seems to describe your life or the life of someone you know.

3. Colón wants young Latinos to take pride in the language of their ancestors. How can people develop pride in their heritage?

4. Colón wants to get rid of the stereotypes of Latinos on television and in films. What stereotypes of Latinos do you think TV and film show?

5. In what ways can stereotypes of people be harmful?

UNDERSTANDING WORDS IN CONTEXT

Read the following sentences from the biography. Think about what each underlined word means. In your notebook, write what the word means as it is used in the sentence.

1. Two Puerto Rican teenagers were walking by the park when they saw a crowd. Intrigued, they walked closer.

2. "The streets are a phenomenal place to play and reach audiences," she says.

3. "I realized all you need is a good play. It doesn't matter who wrote it, as long as it's relevant," Colón says.

4. When Colón founded the theater, she had distinct ideas about her goals. "We wanted bilingual theater. . . . We wanted to emphasize Puerto Rican culture."

5. Colón began a huge fund-raising campaign to transform the old building into a proper theater.

RECALLING DETAILS

1. Give two reasons Colón staged her first performances in parks.

2. Why did she call the company the Puerto Rican Traveling Theatre?

3. How did Colón's mother support her dream to be an actress?

4. Why does the Puerto Rican Traveling Theatre perform in both Spanish and English?

5. What does the Puerto Rican Traveling Theatre do today?

UNDERSTANDING INFERENCES

In your notebook, write two or three sentences that support each of the following inferences.

1. The Puerto Rican Traveling Theatre appeals to people of all cultures.

2. It was clear when Colón was young that she was a talented actress.

3. Colón thinks that theater can help people, not just entertain them.

4. Colón found that operating a traveling theater can be difficult.

5. Colón hopes the Puerto Rican Traveling Theatre will help educate the general public about Latinos.

INTERPRETING WHAT YOU HAVE READ

1. Why do you think Colón believes the streets are a "phenomenal place" to present plays?

2. How can you see the influence of Colón's mother later in her life?

3. Why do you think Colón felt it was necessary to have a building for the theater?

4. Why do you think Colón is so interested in having young Latino playwrights write plays about their experience?

5. Why might Latino playwrights want to depict people with "all their defects and all their virtues"?

ANALYZING QUOTATIONS

Read the following quotation from the biography and answer the questions below.

> "I want Hispanic youngsters to take pride in the language of their parents and at the same time I want to keep those older people in the habit of listening to spoken Spanish literature."

1. How could plays help young Latinos take pride in the language of their parents?

2. Why do you think Colón feels it is important to keep older people listening to Spanish-language plays?

3. Do you think is it important to know the language of your ancestors? Why or why not?

THINKING CRITICALLY

1. How might you keep your culture and the language of your culture alive?

2. Why do you think *The Ox Cart* created such a reaction among the Puerto Ricans who saw it?

3. What qualities do you think Colón has that allowed her to be so successful?

4. What impact do you think the Puerto Rican Traveling Theatre has had in New York?

5. Colón's mother "never pushed me away from the direction I wanted to go." In what ways is it helpful for a parent to guide a child? Explain.

CULTURAL CONNECTIONS

Thinking About What People Do

1. Imagine that you cover the arts for a local newspaper. Write a review of a performance or an art opening that you have just attended. You may review the work of one of the artists in this unit or of another artist whose work you know. Describe what you have seen or heard and give your opinion of the performance or artwork.

2. Pretend that you are one of the subjects interviewed in this unit. Write a letter to someone who helped you in your career that mentions how that person made a difference in your work.

3. Some of the people you read about in this unit changed the kind of work they did. Compare two of these artists and describe their career changes. Then pretend you are an employment counselor and advise that person about how he or she might succeed in the new field.

Thinking About Culture

1. Select two of the people in this unit and think about how their cultural backgrounds influence their work. Which cultural elements do they use in their work? Give examples from the biographies.

2. What kinds of challenges and frustrations did the people in this unit face because of their cultural heritage? In what ways was their heritage an advantage?

Building Research Skills

Work with a partner to complete the following activity.

Look back at the biographies in this unit and choose one career that interests you. Make a list of questions you would like to answer about that career. You might begin your list with the following:

Hint: The Bibliography at the back of this book will give you ideas about books and articles to help you begin your research.

☆ What kinds of talents or skills would I need to pursue this type of work?

☆ How and where could I gain the necessary skills?

☆ What costs might be involved?

☆ Is this type of work done with a group or would I work alone?

Hint: Look for interviews in magazines or newspapers with other people who are successful in this field.

☆ What might be my greatest satisfaction or my biggest sacrifice in this career?

Next, research this career at the library.

Prepare a notebook page that lists the name of the career, the skills and education needed, and the length of time needed to train for this field. Combine your page with those of your classmates to make a Career Notebook. Get some ideas about the kinds of work you might do in the future!

Hint: If you can find someone in your community who works in this field, try to interview that person.

Extending Your Studies

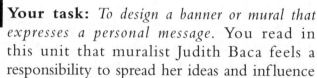

VISUAL ARTS **Your task:** *To design a banner or mural that expresses a personal message.* You read in this unit that muralist Judith Baca feels a responsibility to spread her ideas and influence others through her work. Think of one topic about which you have a strong opinion or choose one of the causes taken up by a person in this unit. Write some phrases expressing this opinion. Then revise your message to a few words. You might choose a message such as "Recycle Now!" or "Shorten the School Week!"

Decorate a piece of cloth or paper with your message. Use bright colors to catch your viewers' attention. If you used an idea from one of the biographies, include a picture that reflects your subject's cultural heritage. Your image might represent, for example, a particular geographical location, climate, food, clothing, art, dance, or scene of family life. Hang your finished artwork in your classroom or school where other students can "get your message."

MATH **Your task:** *To set up a balance sheet that shows a budget for an artistic project.* Some of the people you have read about in this unit manage a company or center that allows them to exhibit their work. These are run as a business, with funds coming in as well as going out.

Work with a small group to imagine your own artistic company. What kind of artistic work will you present? What will be your company name? Write a list of possible expenses. Estimate your costs as closely as you can. For example, will you need to pay for any of the following?

☆ costumes	☆ stage construction
☆ music	☆ advertising
☆ lighting	☆ programs and tickets
☆ art materials	☆ lighting

Now think with your group about the money that you might take in from this project. Will you sell tickets to a performance? Will you sell a finished product, such as a book of poetry or a painted T-shirt? Will some money come from donations? Write a list of the possible amounts and sources of your income.

Place your income and expenses lists next to each other and compare them. Your two lists should "balance," or be even, on both sides.

GEOGRAPHY **Your task:** *To create a picture postcard.* Choose one country from Latin America that you would like to learn about. Think of information that a visitor might want to know, such as climate, holidays, customs, attractions, and location. Look up these facts and take notes about the information you find.

Look for pictures in reference books about your country. Cut words and photographs from old magazines or draw them yourself. Arrange your pictures on oaktag or construction paper in the form of a large "postcard." Write some of your facts in a lively way to interest your reader. Convince your classmates to visit your country.

Write your room number and school address on your postcard. Make a class display or set up the postcards in a "Wish You Were Here" file. Invite other students to visit your "travel agency" and ask them to choose their favorite destination.

WRITING WORKSHOP

As you know, a biography is the true story of a person's life. In this lesson, you will write a **biographical sketch of someone you know**—a classmate or someone about your own age. Since your biography will be a "sketch" of the person you choose, do not try to cover the person's entire life. Just think about one event or situation that shows something about this person. Then write your sketch to introduce your subject to the class.

PREWRITING

Begin your biographical sketch with one or more of these **prewriting** methods. Choose a friend or classmate with whom you have shared an experience. Think through the details of the experience so you can present a clear picture to your readers. It might help if you look at photographs or other souvenirs. You might also talk with your friend to jog your memory about details.

Select someone who interests you and who you feel would interest others. You may want to choose two or three subjects, review what you know about each person and the experience you shared, then narrow your selection.

Once you have selected the subject and the experience you will relate, you can continue your prewriting activities. Here are two suggestions:

List details: Write a detailed list that describes the person, the event, and your feelings about them. Write quickly whatever comes to mind, without trying to form sentences. Think about these questions:

☆ What happened?

☆ Where did the experience take place?

☆ What sounds did you hear?

☆ How did the place look?

☆ What did your subject do or say?

☆ How did he or she react?

☆ What did you learn about the subject from this experience?

☆ What did you learn about yourself?

Go through the questions one by one and write descriptive answers. Include details from all five senses. The details will help you draw a precise picture of your subject.

Freewriting: Read over the words and ideas you listed. Select one detail that appeals to you and start writing. Do not choose your words carefully at this point; just write freely for two minutes. Your freewriting will help you compose a word sketch of your subject.

Organizing: Now that you have begun to describe your subject, you can organize your material. Arrange your notes so that they are useful to you. You might sort details by the senses, for example, or use space order or time order as your guide.

DRAFTING

Once you have your details and freewriting phrases organized, you can begin **drafting** your biographical sketch.

Consider the story behind the story: Think about why you selected this experience. As you write, add details to show what changes occurred in your subject and how it affected you. The more you personalize your writing and make it meaningful to you, the more you will please your readers.

Keep the structure simple: Do not let your readers become confused. Relate the incident in a straightforward manner. Make sure your sketch has a beginning, a middle, and an end.

REVISING

Put your sketch aside for a day or two. Then, with the help of another student who will act as your editor, evaluate and **revise** your work. See the directions for writers and student editors below.

Directions for Writers: Before you give your work to your classmate to edit, check it over yourself. Read it aloud to hear how it sounds. Then ask yourself such questions as these:

☆ Does the opening catch my reader's interest?

☆ Do I give enough interesting details to describe the event well?

☆ Does the dialogue sound like real speech?

☆ Am I *showing*, not *telling*, the reader what happened?

☆ Does the ending sum up what I have learned?

Make notes for your next draft or revise your writing before you give it to a student editor. Then ask your student editor to read your work. Listen carefully to his or her suggestions. If they seem helpful, use them to improve your writing when you revise your work.

Directions for Student Editors: Read the work carefully and respectfully, remembering that your purpose is to help the writer do his or her best work. Keep in mind that an editor should always make positive, helpful comments that point to specific parts of the sketch. After you have read the work, use these questions to help you direct your comments:

☆ What did I like most about the biographical sketch?

☆ Can I picture the person or event in my mind?

☆ Do I feel that I know the subject?

☆ Has the writer used enough details to describe the subject clearly?

☆ What did the writer learn about his or her subject?

☆ What would I like to know more about?

PROOFREADING

When you are satisfied that your work says what you want it to say, **proofread** it for errors in spelling, punctuation, capitalization, and grammar. Then make a neat, final copy of your biographical sketch.

PUBLISHING

After you revise and proofread your writing, you are ready to **publish** or share it. Put together a classroom portrait gallery called Someone You Should Know and display the biographical sketches for your classmates to read.

LATINOS IN THE SCIENCES AND MATHEMATICS

In this unit, you will read about five Latinos who have made contributions to the sciences and mathematics. Think about how their enthusiasm and dedication led to their success. As you read, give special attention to the way these people's cultural heritage helped them achieve their goals.

According to Bolivian American teacher **Jaime Escalante** (es-kah-LAHN-teh), "The only thing you need [to succeed] . . . is *ganas* [desire]." Escalante inspires his high school calculus students to pass demanding exams.

Venezuelan American conservationist **Francisco Dallmeier** (DAHL-may-er) thinks that rain forests can be saved through education. He notes, "It's rewarding to see [local people] get into important positions in their countries."

Experiencing a painful illness as a child in Puerto Rico helped **Antonia Novello** (noh-VEH-yoh) prepare to be Surgeon General of the United States: "My pediatrician was kind. I wanted to be a doctor like him."

Born to Mexican parents, author and psychologist **Clarissa Pinkola Estés** (pihn-KOH-lah ES-tes) feels that by listening to the stories people tell about their lives, "I became related to living poets and their work."

Originally from Colombia, **Adriana Ocampo** (oh-KAHM-poh) is a planetary geologist for NASA. She thinks that North and South America should share their knowledge about space. "You have to look at things globally," she says.

As you read the biographies in this unit, try to identify some of the qualities that helped these people succeed in their fields. Think also about how the childhood experiences of each of these individuals have contributed to their choice of career.

JAIME ESCALANTE

Jaime Escalante teaches mathematics to a high school class. Escalante combined his experience teaching in Bolivia and the United States to conclude that all students can be successful in math. They only need to bring to class a desire to learn.

The teenagers were talking and chasing one another when math teacher Jaime Escalante (HEYE-meh es-kah-LAHN-teh) walked into his first class at Garfield High School in East Los Angeles. They stared at him with hard looks. He stared back, dismayed by their language, and their anger, and was even, perhaps, a little afraid of them. In despair, he wondered if he could stand a year here.

Garfield High was in trouble. Gangs seemed to run the school and little learning went on. Hundreds of students dropped out every year. Most of the teachers seemed to have given up. After the shock wore off at what he found at Garfield, Escalante came to realize that the students were not to blame. No one was expecting anything of them.

"They were using their fingers adding stuff at the board," he says of the students. "They came in without supplies, with nothing. Total chaos."[1]

He painted his classroom and put up pictures of sports stars. He tried reaching the teenagers with humor, wearing a chef's apron and bringing a cleaver[2] to class to chop apples and explain fractions. He appealed to their heritage. "The Mayans were way ahead of everybody on the concept of zero; you *burros* have math in your blood!"

Bit by bit, he became known for his sense of fun and his tough standards. But no one at the school was prepared when he announced in 1978 that he was going to teach an Advanced Placement (AP) calculus class and have the students take the AP calculus test at the end of the year. Only 2 percent of high school seniors in the country take this difficult test, but those who pass it earn college credit. For someone from Garfield to take any AP test was rare. For Escalante to turn these kids into calculus

---

1. **chaos** (KAY-ahs) *n.* a state of complete confusion
2. **cleaver** (KLEE-vuhr) *n.* a large knife used for cutting meat

whizzes seemed impossible. That first year he had fourteen students, but only five lasted the year. One passed the AP test.

Another teacher might have given up and agreed that the kids were hopeless. Escalante's failure only made him more determined. As he often told his students, "The only thing you need to have for my program—and you must bring it every day—is *ganas* (GAH-nahs)," the Spanish word for *desire*. He begged money for summer calculus courses and he searched the junior high schools for students. In 1979, nine students signed up for AP calculus. Six passed. In 1980, fifteen students took the class and fourteen passed.

"I often chose the rascals and kids who were discipline problems, as well as those who simply liked math," Escalante says. "I found that the class cut-ups were often the most intelligent." His approach worked. People started to take notice of this odd success story in a school that before had been known only for gangs and trouble.

In 1981, he had 18 students. By now, Escalante was a legend at the school. A gang member in one class nicknamed him Kimo. "Kemo Sabe, like the Lone Ranger," the student explained to Escalante. It was the boy's favorite show. To him, and the other students, it meant someone who was Spanish and someone who was wise. The name stuck.

The 1981 AP calculus class worked harder than they had ever worked in their lives. They lived, slept, and breathed calculus. They came in at 7 A.M., stayed after school, and went to class Saturday mornings. Then disaster struck. Escalante was in class when his eyes suddenly would not work and he felt a sharp pain. He left class and fell down a flight of stairs.

When he awoke, he was in a hospital. Before the doctors could even tell what was wrong, Escalante had gone back to his students. All this made the legend grow. He was about to die, the students whispered, and Kimo had dragged himself out of bed to come to school. If he did that, they vowed, they could at least study. The real story was that Escalante had gallstones. Later that year, the attacks resumed, and he had his gallbladder removed.

When the AP calculus results came back, every one of the 18 students had passed. This was remarkable for any school, but almost unbelievable for an inner-city school like Garfield. Those at the Advanced Placement testing service didn't believe it, either. They accused[3] 14 of the students of cheating.

Escalante was furious, but finally agreed to have the students take the test again. Every one of the 12 students (two could not take the retest) passed. It was this story that interested Hollywood and became the movie *Stand and Deliver,* based on what Escalante had done at Garfield. (See the biography of Edward James Olmos, who played Escalante in the movie, on page 81.) Perhaps most important to Escalante, his sister in Bolivia heard the story of Garfield's AP calculus triumph[4] on the "Voice of America," a radio program that transmits[5] news from the United States. She began to cry with happiness. She couldn't wait to tell their mother about Jaime's success. He had left Bolivia with great dreams. Now, it seemed, he had accomplished them.

Escalante was born in Bolivia in 1930. He grew up in the remote Indian village of Achacachi (ah-chah-KAH-cheh), where his schoolteacher parents had been assigned[6] to teach. When he was nine, his mother left his father and took the children to live in La Paz. His mother continued to work as a teacher, scraping together enough money for Jaime to attend a private Catholic school. Even then, he enjoyed a reputation for stunts that sometimes got him into trouble. Once, when a handball disappeared down a drainage pipe high on a wall, Escalante climbed a rickety[7] ladder to find out where it had gone. In his eagerness to see what else was up there, he stayed too long. The ladder collapsed and Escalante was left with a broken arm.

Perhaps because of his lifelong love of mischief, Escalante understood kids. Like his parents, Escalante became a teacher. Soon his tricks and success with students made him one of the best-known teachers in Bolivia. As he did later in the United

---

3. **accused** (uh-KYOOZD) *v.* charged with an offense
4. **triumph** (TREYE-uhmf) *n.* great success
5. **transmits** (tranz-MIHTS) *v.* broadcasts
6. **assigned** (uh-SEYEND) *v.* appointed to a job
7. **rickety** (RIHK-iht-ee) *adj.* shaky; likely to fall or break

States, Escalante spent endless hours with them and turned math into a game. But finally, the low salary of Bolivian teachers and the political uncertainty became too great. In 1963, Jaime Escalante and his wife and son moved to the United States. (See **Did You Know?** on page 123 for more information about Bolivian political history.)

Escalante's first job in his new country was washing dishes. That didn't bother him. He didn't know much English. "No problem," he told his wife Fabiola. He would learn English, send in his teaching credentials,[8] and then he could teach. The state of California disagreed. His Bolivian credentials were not valid in the United States. If he wanted to teach in this country, he had to earn another college degree—and spend another year after that to get a master's degree. He was devastated. All those years of teaching? The awards? Did they mean nothing?

Escalante's response was to follow the advice that he always wrote on posters on the walls where he taught: DETERMINATION + HARD WORK + DISCIPLINE = SUCCESS. For seven long, hard years he worked as a busboy, a cook, and an electronics factory worker, all the while going to college at night. The easy thing may have been to return to Bolivia. After all, he already had a reputation there. But as the Escalantes spent time in the United States, they found it harder and harder to leave. Education was critical, they believed, and in this country, their sons Jaimito and Fernando could get the best education.

Escalante has not regretted this decision. He has become nationally known for his teaching skills—then-President Reagan called him a "national treasure" on television. Since Escalante began the emphasis on AP programs, Garfield has continued them. In 1989, more than 450 AP tests in 16 subjects were given to Garfield students.

Escalante is now teaching high school in Sacramento, California. He wants to show that his success can be repeated.

---

8. **credentials** (krih-DEHN-shuhlz) *n. pl.* papers that show a person is qualified to do something

His belief in teenagers remains strong. "When hard work is combined with love, humor, and a recognition of the *ganas*—the desire to learn—the stereotypes and the barriers begin to crumble."

> **Did You Know?** *There was considerable unrest during the early 1960s in Bolivia. The Nationalistic Revolutionary Movement (NMR) took control of the government in 1952, and the economy was in a state of upheaval. After Escalante emigrated in 1963, his feelings about the instability of the government were proven correct. The NMR was overthrown by the military in 1964. Between 1964 and 1982, the government was overthrown several times. In 1982, some stability returned with the inauguration of President Hernán Siles Zuazo (SWA-soh), when the military returned the country to civil rule.*

AFTER YOU READ

EXPLORING YOUR RESPONSES

1. Do you think that the students at Garfield were to blame for their poor performance? Why or why not?

2. Think of something in your life that you needed *ganas*—desire—to accomplish. How did that desire help you accomplish your goal?

3. Imagine that you had been one of the students accused of cheating on the AP calculus test. What might your response have been?

4. How do you think Escalante's teaching methods could help his students outside his class?

5. Escalante posted his formula for success on the walls of his classrooms. What is your formula for success?

UNDERSTANDING WORDS IN CONTEXT

Read the following sentences from the biography. Think about what each underlined word means. In your notebook, write what the word means as it is used in the sentence.

1. "They came in without supplies, with nothing. Total chaos."

2. Perhaps most important to Escalante, his sister in Bolivia heard the story of Garfield's AP calculus triumph on the "Voice of America," a radio program that transmits news from the United States.

3. He grew up in the remote Indian village of Achacachi, where his schoolteacher parents had been assigned to teach.

4. Escalante climbed a rickety ladder to find out where [a ball] had gone. In his eagerness to see what else was up there, he stayed too long. The ladder collapsed.

5. He would learn English, send in his teaching <u>credentials</u>, and then he could teach.

RECALLING DETAILS

1. Why were people surprised when Escalante said he would be teaching an AP calculus class at Garfield?

2. Why did Escalante often choose what he called the "rascals and kids with discipline problems" to be in his AP calculus class?

3. Why did the AP testing service accuse the Garfield calculus students of cheating?

4. What did Escalante have to do if he wanted to teach in the United States?

5. Why does Escalante believe that he is so successful with high school students?

UNDERSTANDING INFERENCES

In your notebook, write two or three sentences from the biography that support each of the following inferences.

1. Jaime Escalante was correct in his ideas about his students' abilities.

2. Humor can help people learn.

3. Escalante often chose students for his AP classes who were similar to the way he was as a student.

4. Education was always important to Jaime Escalante and his family.

5. Once Escalante began proving that Garfield students could achieve, others at the school began to believe it.

INTERPRETING WHAT YOU HAVE READ

1. Describe a typical class at Garfield High before Escalante arrived.

2. Why do you think that Escalante told his classes about the Mayans' use of math?

3. Why do you think Escalante believed that the students at Garfield High could do calculus?

4. Why do you think that Escalante's students were willing to work so hard for him?

5. What qualities make Escalante such a good teacher?

ANALYZING QUOTATIONS

Read the following quotation from the biography and answer the questions below.

"When hard work is combined with love, humor, and a recognition of the ganas—the desire to learn—the stereotypes and the barriers begin to crumble."

1. Why do you think Escalante believes that hard work can destroy stereotypes?

2. What does this quotation say about Escalante's relationship with his students?

3. How can learning break down barriers?

THINKING CRITICALLY

1. What characteristics do you think helped Escalante become so successful with his students?

2. Why do you think that Escalante decided to begin an AP calculus class at Garfield High?

3. Do you agree with Escalante that class cut-ups are often intelligent? Why or why not?

4. Do you think Escalante liked the nickname Kimo? Why or why not?

5. Think of three good teachers you have had. What did they have in common?

FRANCISCO DALLMEIER

Venezuelan American researcher Francisco Dallmeier investigates an animal skeleton he found in his explorations of the rain forests of the world. Dallmeier hopes to save rain forests by educating people about their importance.

Francisco Dallmeier (DAHL-may-er) was in a remote rain forest in Peru doing research when he noticed that one of his research teams hadn't come back. The boat pilot came to Dallmeier, worried. "Listen," he said, "I went to get those people and they weren't there."

Dallmeier decided to take two guides who knew the area and search for the missing scientists. The guides led the way, hacking at the thick underbrush with machetes. "Once we got deeper into the forest, it started raining very badly, a tropical rain shower," Dallmeier says. It was impossible to see. The marks the group members had made to find their way back washed away. The sky was black. Dallmeier and his guides were lost.

Dallmeier had learned survival techniques during his training to become a pilot. "I had learned that once you get lost you stay where you are. Instead of getting desperate you calm down and regroup. I asked one of [the guides] to get some palm leaves and start making a little roof to protect us from the weather. I sent the other guy to get firewood from the bottom parts of dead trees." The guides watched, astonished, as Dallmeier pulled a flashlight out of his pack and the equipment to build a fire. The temperature was warm—80° to 85°—but the fire would help dry soaked clothes and boots. As the fire began to blaze, Dallmeier pulled out granola bars and peanuts. "It was better than the food in camp," he says.

Finally, the three fell asleep under the palm leaf tent, but at about 3 A.M., one of the guides woke up. A vampire bat had bitten his toe. Blood was streaming everywhere. "After that, I sat by the fire and waited until morning," Dallmeier says. The next morning, they went to the river, where "eventually, one of the boats came by. It wasn't that bad. I was ready." The missing scientists were found, too, and Dallmeier returned to his work. "I try not to tell too many stories like that. This is a great job."

In many ways, a life spent exploring forests is Dallmeier's dream job. He was born in Caracas, Venezuela, in 1954 to a German mother and a Venezuelan father. (See **Did You Know?** on page 132 for more information about the European cultures that contributed to Venezuelan history and culture.) His great-grandfather founded the botanic gardens in Venezuela and the biology school of the Central University of Venezuela. "They'd always tell me I was going to be like my great-grandfather," says Dallmeier, whose love for anything green became apparent early. His family felt most at home in the city, but Dallmeier spent his time trying to find ways to head to the wild. He joined the Boy Scouts so he could go camping, and whenever he could he chased butterflies and bugs for his collection. Every summer, his family took a month's vacation at the beach. Once they arrived, Dallmeier took off on his own. He would spend all his free time exploring. "That was wonderful. It was really my only experience staying in a remote area and freely running around, doing whatever I wanted."

In high school in Caracas, "I wanted to start working at the Museum of Natural History, but they didn't allow me in. I was just a baby." After constant begging, the museum let him work afternoons and nights when he was 13. He started by cleaning the museum. By the time he was in his second year of college at the Central University of Venezuela, he was the director of the museum. "In college, professors were impressed by how much I knew about birds and animals."

When Dallmeier graduated in 1979, he began working for an international firm that wrote environmental impact statements. These reports explained how a construction project or factory would affect the environment. "I really learned the concept of time being money," Dallmeier says. "I wasn't used to that." Instead, Dallmeier notes that in straight scientific research there is a sense of having all the time in the world to complete an experiment or project. Although he enjoyed the work, after four years, writing reports became too routine. He began to look for more challenges.

Dallmeier decided he wanted to do graduate work in science, and was accepted at Colorado State University. "I sold my apartment, got rid of all my possessions. It was a hard transition,[1] to go from having a salary and traveling to becoming a student where you have to count your pennies." Dallmeier felt that he had to get his doctorate[2] to go any further, though. "In science if you don't have a Ph.D. you're not really there."

Because most of his college texts had been written in English, Dallmeier could read and write the language. Speaking it was more difficult. The only discrimination he saw was when non-native speakers mispronounced English. "Sometimes if you don't speak clearly, people don't think you're very intelligent," he says.

While at Colorado State, he met Joy Parton, the woman he would marry in 1985. The next year he earned his doctorate. He also wrote a book about wildlife ecology. "I knew I wanted to work internationally. That was my goal."

Dallmeier was offered several jobs. The most exciting one was at the Smithsonian Institution. There, the new Man and the Biosphere[3] Biological Diversity[4] Program needed a director. The purpose of the program is to study how people interact with their natural environment and to find ways to protect the places where people are threatening the environment. The job meant traveling often to different parts of the world, which was also appealing. Dallmeier took the job and still heads the program for the Smithsonian.

Since Dallmeier became director, he has focused on what has been happening to rain forests around the world. He is trying to find ways to stop the destruction. To do that, he and his teams go to countries to research what is occurring. Then the scientists try to show the country's people what effects the destruction is

1. **transition** (tran-ZIH-shuhn) *n.* a movement from one condition to another
2. **doctorate** (DAHK-tuh-ruht) *n.* the rank or title of doctor, or Ph.D., earned after years of academic study and research after college
3. **biosphere** (BEYE-uh-sfihr) *n.* all of the living things of the Earth together with their environment
4. **diversity** (duh-VUHR-suh-tee) *n.* variety

having, and explain how they can use the rain forests without destroying them. "We've worked in almost every country in Latin America, as well as China, Taiwan, Indonesia, Malaysia, and this year, Africa," he says.

Although Dallmeier and his team try to document[5] and slow the destruction of the rain forests, "We are working with a handful of people, and there are thousands of people against us." He does feel that he can have an impact by teaching people how important it is to protect the rain forests. "It's rewarding to see them get into important positions in their countries and have them thank you for the knowledge you gave them," he says. Dallmeier figures that there are about 600 people around the world he has trained. Recently, he ran into a man from Nigeria whom he had taught. "Now he's director of a biodiversity program in Nigeria," Dallmeier says with satisfaction. He is hopeful that in Nigeria, at least, there is someone in power who can slow the destruction.

Being born in Venezuela—and speaking Spanish and Portuguese as well as English—can be a help. "In my case, I can play that I'm Venezuelan, which helps in many Latin countries. In other countries being American helps me to understand their culture better and meet their demands. I feel I am American, but because of my background I don't totally belong to one country. No matter where I go, someone always asks me where I'm from. I just have to learn to live with that." Dallmeier has become a U.S. citizen, though. "I really love this country," he says. "This is the best country in the world."

More difficult than a shifting sense of identity is traveling to areas with living conditions that would bother most Americans. "It's dangerous flying in some of these small planes," he notes. The equipment can be poor, and people sometimes share the floor with chickens and other animals. Dallmeier says that having two colleagues[6] die on such planes last year has made him more cautious. "Sometimes, though, there's no other choice," he adds.

---

5. **document** (DAH-kyoo-muhnt) *v.* to record; to find evidence of
6. **colleagues** (KAHL-eegz) *n. pl.* people who do the same kind of work

At times, Dallmeier has had to negotiate with shaky military governments. Once, in Ecuador, Dallmeier stayed in a house that, two days later, housed rebel guerrilla[7] fighters from Peru. "I've interacted with drug dealers, coca growers," he says. "It's all part of the job." Even though vampire bats and drug dealers are part of the job, the ability to make a difference in the health of the earth is a reward Dallmeier wouldn't give up for anything.

> **Did You Know?** *Like many other countries in North and South America, Venezuela was a target for European explorers. The Italian explorer Christopher Columbus sailed into what is now the Gulf of Paria in 1498. German adventurers did most of the European exploring in Venezuela, but the Spaniards colonized the country. By the 1520s, there were Spanish settlements on the coast. Venezuela was considered a Spanish property until 1810, when Venezuelan Simón Bolívar (boh-LEE-vahr) led a successful war for independence. Many Europeans also fled to Venezuela to escape the destruction of World War II.*

---

7. **guerrilla** (guh-RIHL-uh) *adj.* a soldier who doesn't belong to a regular army; guerrillas often fight their enemy by making quick, surprise attacks

AFTER YOU READ

EXPLORING YOUR RESPONSES

1. Imagine you are Francisco Dallmeier and one of your teams is missing in the Peruvian rain forest. What might you do?

2. Would you enjoy Dallmeier's job? Why or why not?

3. Dallmeier loved the outdoors as a child. What do you enjoy doing now that might help you in your career?

4. Dallmeier says he has noticed that people discriminate against those who mispronounce English. What other things cause people to discriminate against others?

5. Would you like a job in which you were constantly traveling? What would be the best and worst parts of a job like that?

UNDERSTANDING WORDS IN CONTEXT

Read the following sentences from the biography. Think about what each underlined word means. In your notebook, write what the word means as it is used in the sentence.

1. "It was a hard transition, to go from having a salary and traveling to becoming a student where you have to count your pennies."

2. Dallmeier felt he had to get his doctorate to go any further, though. "In science if you don't have a Ph.D. you're not really there."

3. There, the new Man and the Biosphere Biological Diversity Program needed a director. The purpose of this program is to study how people interact with their natural environment.

4. Although Dallmeier and his team try to document and slow the destruction of the rain forests, "We are working with a handful of people, and there are thousands of people against us."

5. Once, in Ecuador, Dallmeier stayed in a house that, two days later, housed rebel <u>guerrilla</u> fighters from Peru.

RECALLING DETAILS

1. What did Dallmeier learn that helped him survive in the Peruvian rain forest?

2. Why did his family tell him he was going to be like his great-grandfather?

3. Why did the Museum of Natural History make Dallmeier its director while he was still in college?

4. How was writing environmental impact statements different from the research Dallmeier had done?

5. Explain the research that Dallmeier does.

UNDERSTANDING INFERENCES

In your notebook, write two or three sentences from the biography that support each of the following inferences.

1. As a child, Dallmeier's interests were very different from those of his family.

2. Dallmeier found ways to follow his interests.

3. Dallmeier has been willing to give up comfortable situations to accomplish what he wanted.

4. A group or even one person working on his own can help save the rain forests.

5. Understanding the viewpoints of people from different countries is an advantage in Dallmeier's job.

INTERPRETING WHAT YOU HAVE READ

1. How do you think Dallmeier reacts to dangerous situations in his job?

2. What in Dallmeier's background made him so sought-after when he looked for a job after earning his doctorate?

3. How important do you think Dallmeier's cultural background is to him?

4. Why do you think Dallmeier chose to work in the Man and the Biosphere Biological Diversity Program?

5. What do you think Dallmeier would like to see happen as a result of his work?

ANALYZING QUOTATIONS

Read the following quotation from the story and answer the questions below.

> *"I feel I am American, but because of my background I don't totally belong to one country. No matter where I go, someone always asks me where I'm from. I just have to learn to live with that."*

1. Why would Dallmeier's background make him feel he doesn't belong completely to the United States?

2. How do you think Dallmeier feels about not completely belonging to one country?

3. What are the advantages and disadvantages of belonging to a country?

THINKING CRITICALLY

1. Francisco Dallmeier believes that his work has made a difference. Explain why you agree or disagree.

2. What do you think is the most difficult part of Dallmeier's job? Explain your answer.

3. Do you think Dallmeier is optimistic or pessimistic about the fate of the world? Why do you think so?

4. How might Dallmeier's career have been different if he had been born and raised in the United States?

5. Dallmeier considers his work important. What other kinds of work might help change the world?

ANTONIA NOVELLO

Former Surgeon General of the United States, Antonia Novello, testifies before the Senate Labor and Resources Committee at her confirmation hearing in February, 1990. Born in Puerto Rico, Novello was the first woman and the first Latino to serve as Surgeon General.

Antonia Novello (noh–VEH–yoh) was born Antonia Coello (koh–EH–yoh) in Fajardo (fah–HAHR–doh), Puerto Rico, in 1944. Her colon[1] was oversized, and it didn't work well. The condition was painful. "I was hospitalized every summer for at least two weeks," she remembers. But because her mother never treated her as someone to be pitied, Novello didn't pity herself. "I was a sick kid, but my mother never made me feel sick. Life issues you a card, and you have to learn to play it."

Novello has played her card well. From 1990 to 1992, she served as Surgeon General of the United States, one of the most important jobs in medicine. The Surgeon General is seen as the "doctor for all Americans," the person who speaks out on national health problems and how they might be solved.

When Novello was 8 years old, she was told she needed surgery to correct her colon condition. The surgery was not performed for ten years. "Somebody forgot," she says. "The university hospital was in the north. I was 32 miles away, my mother (who was a school principal) could only take me on Saturday, so the surgery was never done. I do believe that some people fall through the cracks. I was one of those."

The years of pain did have one good effect. "My pediatrician[2] was kind. I wanted to be a doctor like him." Another doctor was dean of the medical school, "and all my life his was the hand I saw—soothing and caring. My favorite aunt was my nurse, and she always said, 'You have to be a doctor, so that I can work with you.'"

Novello kept those ideas to herself, although she dreamed of becoming a doctor for the children in her hometown. "I never

---

1. **colon** (KOH-luhn) *n.* the lower part of the large intestine
2. **pediatrician** (pee-dee-uh-TRIH-shuhn) *n.* a doctor who treats children

told anyone that I wanted to be that. It seemed too grand a notion," she says. "After all, I was a little girl from a little town." She also wanted to become a doctor to make sure that others would not fall through the cracks as she had. "I thought, when I grow up, no other person is going to wait 18 years for surgery."

Throughout her childhood, Novello kept her dream of becoming a doctor alive, even though her family was not wealthy. Her father had died when she was 8 years old.

Novello was 18 years old when she insisted that her painful condition be corrected. Only one doctor, a heart surgeon, was willing to operate. Novello had to leave Puerto Rico and miss school for a semester to travel to the Mayo Clinic in Minnesota.

During her senior year in college at the University of Puerto Rico, she applied to medical school without telling anyone. Just as she kept the idea of becoming a doctor to herself when she was young, now her sense of insecurity kept her quiet again. Despite her mother's encouragement, that support wasn't enough to counteract[3] Novello's insecurity. She explains it as "the typical attitude of women at that time—fear of failure."

Once she was accepted to medical school, her mother told her not to worry about the cost. "Mommy never panicked. When I told her I was accepted to medical school she said that as long as there is a bank out there we will find your tuition."

Her mother's determination helped carry Novello through her years of medical school at the University of Puerto Rico. "I wasn't allowed to work until I graduated from medical school because my mother felt that once I earned money I might be sidetracked by material rewards before I got to my real work."

While she was in medical school, Novello had more surgery and missed a semester. "I survived many times in my life by learning to laugh at myself—that's the best medicine. But I also became very self-assured and capable."

Novello excelled in medical school. In 1970, the year she graduated, she married another doctor, Joseph Novello. They

---

3. **counteract** (kown-tuhr-AKT) *v.* to cancel; offset

moved to Michigan, where both continued their medical studies. The next year, Novello was the first woman to receive the Intern of the Year award at the University of Michigan's pediatric department. "It was difficult for women to be accepted [in medicine] then, and I always was impressed with the way she handled situations," says fellow intern Dr. Samuel Sefton.

Novello believes that her early experience with illness gives her a deep sympathy with her patients. She is "very conscious of how people feel when they are in the bed as a patient," she says.

"Another thing that 20 years of disease did to me is that I have very little tolerance[4] for people who complain of being sick and truly are not. And I have very little tolerance for people who say they can't do something or they can't get to the top, because believe me, if I did it . . . it can be done."

Novello opened her own medical practice, but found herself too sympathetic with her patients. "When the pediatrician cries as much as the parents [of patients] do, then you know it's time to get out."

Since then, her career has been in public health. In public health, doctors do everything from researching disease to providing care for people who would not otherwise have access to doctors. Novello joined the Public Health Service in Maryland in 1978 to work with the artificial kidney program there. In 1986, she was named Deputy Director of the National Institute of Child Health and Human Development. Novello felt she had reached the top of her profession. Among other tasks, she supervised national pediatric AIDS research. At the same time, she was a professor of pediatrics at Georgetown University Hospital in Washington, D.C.

Then, in 1989, President George Bush asked Novello to become the first woman, first Puerto Rican, and first Latino Surgeon General of the United States. The Surgeon General heads the Public Health Service, which employs 6,400 medical officers. As the highest official in public health, the Surgeon

---

4. **tolerance** (TAH-luh-ruhnts) *n.* patience; sympathy

General can serve as an advocate[5] for national health concerns. "As a woman, as a minority," she says, "I hope I bring a lot of sensitivity to the job."

Novello returned to Puerto Rico shortly after she became Surgeon General. "When I got off the plane, kids from my mother's school lined both sides of the road handing me flowers." Suddenly, she had become a symbol. "I realized that for these people, for women, I have to be good as a doctor. I have to be good as a Surgeon General. I have to be everything."

While she was Surgeon General, Novello focused on warning young Americans about the dangers of smoking, drinking, and AIDS. "I know if I make good sense and I'm understood, people might be willing to make some changes." Her approach is based on keeping her message simple. While some people may think that simple is bad, "I find it means that you are clever, because in the long run, people will remember your message. That is my quest."[6] One effective way of getting that message across is humor. As she learned when she was young, laughter can go a long way toward smoothing rough edges.

In 1991, Novello took on the makers of wine and beer. Through speeches, she sent the message that their TV advertising encouraged children to start drinking. "The ads have youth believing that instead of getting up early, exercising, going to school, playing a sport, or learning to be a team player, all they have to do to fit in is learn to drink the right alcohol," she says.

Novello also decided to speak out against teenage smoking. "More than 3,000 teenagers begin to smoke each day." If that continues, she says, "then at least five million children now living in the United States will die of smoking-related diseases."

Novello relies on her husband of 24 years for emotional support. Also, she says, "Not having children probably helped because I don't feel so torn between kids who are at home and taking care of all the kids out there."

---

5. **advocate** (AD-vuh-kuht) *n.* a defender
6. **quest** (KWEHST) *n.* a crusade; intention

When President Clinton was elected, Novello was appointed as the United Nations Children's Fund (UNICEF) Special Representative for Health and Nutrition for Women, Children, and Youth. In her new job, Novello is a global leader working toward the immunization of the world's children and the prevention of alcohol, tobacco, and other drug abuse.

In 1990, Novello was named head of a national committee on Latino health care. Fewer Latinos have health insurance than any other group, according to the report. There are also few Latinos in the health care field. Yet another problem is that doctors and health workers often do not understand the differences between Latino groups. They do not understand that a second-generation Puerto Rican from New York City may face different problems than a Mexican American farm worker who was exposed to pesticides. (See *Did You Know?* below for more information about the many different Latino groups.)

As long as she is a doctor, Novello will continue to work for change. "I want to be able to look back someday and say, 'I did make a difference.' Whether it was to open the minds of people to think that a woman can do a good job, or whether it's the fact that so many kids out there think that they could be me, then all the headaches will have been worth it."

> *Did You Know?* The Latinos who live in the United States have many different heritages. About all they have in common is ancestors who came from a Spanish-speaking country. Much of the richness of Latino heritage in Caribbean islands such as Puerto Rico and the Dominican Republic comes from African and native Taino culture. Mexican Americans often have ancestors who were native peoples in Mexico long before the Spanish came, and South Americans often can trace their heritage to other European countries such as Germany. Latinos were all born or grew up somewhere in the Western hemisphere, though, from Alaska south to the tip of Chile.

AFTER YOU READ

EXPLORING YOUR RESPONSES

1. When Novello was young, she thought her dreams of being a doctor were "too grand." Can a person's dreams ever be too grand?

2. Novello's mother didn't want her to work because she was afraid her daughter might be sidetracked by material rewards and not graduate. Do you think this is a danger students face?

3. As Surgeon General, Novello could choose the health problems she brought to the U.S. people. What health issue would you publicize?

4. As the first Latino and the first woman Surgeon General, Novello felt she was a role model. Do you think it would be difficult to be a role model? Explain.

5. Novello believes beer and wine commercials encourage young people to start drinking. Explain why you agree or disagree with her.

UNDERSTANDING WORDS IN CONTEXT

Read the following sentences from the biography. Think about what each underlined word means. In your notebook, write what the word means as it is used in the sentence.

1. "My pediatrician was kind. I wanted to be a doctor like him."

2. Despite her mother's encouragement to go to college, that support wasn't enough to counteract Novello's insecurity.

3. "Another thing that 20 years of disease did to me is that I have very little tolerance for people who complain of being sick and truly are not."

4. As the highest official in public health, the Surgeon General

can serve as an <u>advocate</u> for national health concerns.

5. "I find it means that you are clever, because in the long run, people will remember your message. That is my <u>quest</u>."

RECALLING DETAILS

1. What did Novello learn from her years of illness?
2. Why did Novello want to become a doctor?
3. How did her illness help her develop sympathy for her patients?
4. What was Novello's focus when she was Surgeon General?
5. What are Novello's techniques for getting across her message?

UNDERSTANDING INFERENCES

In your notebook, write two or three sentences from the biography that support each of the following inferences.

1. When she was a young person, Novello was unsure of her abilities.
2. Novello has little patience for excuses.
3. Novello preferred work in public health to having her own medical practice.
4. Antonia Novello sees herself as a role model for Latinos and for women.
5. Novello is not afraid to offend powerful people.

INTERPRETING WHAT YOU HAVE READ

1. What qualities made Novello a good choice for Surgeon General?
2. What qualities does Novello have in common with her mother?
3. How could entering public health help Novello fulfill her childhood reasons for becoming a doctor?

4. How can the Surgeon General make an impact on people's health throughout the United States?

5. How has being Puerto Rican affected Novello's professional life?

ANALYZING QUOTATIONS

Read the following quotation from the biography and answer the questions below.

> *"I want to be able to look back someday and say, 'I did make a difference.' Whether it was to open the minds of people to think that a woman can do a good job, or whether it's the fact that so many kids out there think that they could be me, then all the headaches will have been worth it."*

1. What does it mean to "make a difference"?

2. Why is it so important to Novello to make a difference, and not just to be a good doctor?

3. Do you think it is important to feel you are making a difference? Why or why not?

THINKING CRITICALLY

1. Novello says she never pitied herself when she was a child. How do you think this made a difference in her life?

2. Novello says she has "little tolerance for people who say they can't do something." Explain why you agree or disagree with this idea.

3. Do you think it was difficult for Novello to go against alcohol and cigarette manufacturers? Explain your answer.

4. Do you think Novello has made a difference? Why or why not?

5. What quality of Novello's do you most admire? Why?

CLARISSA PINKOLA ESTÉS

In the best seller *Women Who Run with the Wolves*, psychologist Clarissa Pinkola Estés draws on her Mexican heritage to help her explain how folktales and fairy tales can help people understand themselves and their culture.

"**T**he river *always* called to be visited after dark," author and psychologist[1] Clarissa Pinkola Estés (pihn-KOH-lah ES-tes) writes of her childhood, "the fields *needed* to be walked in so they could make their rustle-talk. Fires *needed* to be built in the forest at night, and stories *needed* to be told outside the hearing of grown-ups."

Pinkola Estés thinks that telling stories is the way for people to understand who they are. For 20 years, she wrote stories that explained why people do what they do. She tried to get them published, only to be turned down time after time. When she finally found a publisher, her book *Women Who Run with the Wolves* came out, in 1992, with very little notice.

Then something happened. People bought it and told their friends to buy it. In this way, hundreds of thousands of copies have been sold. Pinkola Estés is a celebrity who receives hundreds of letters a week and who gets mobbed when she arrives at readings. She is a publishing phenomenon.[2]

It is a happy ending to a story that has taken many odd turns. Pinkola Estés was born in Michigan in 1943 to Mexican migrant workers[3] named Estés. (See **Did You Know?** on page 150 for more information about Mexican migrant workers.) They taught her to speak Spanish, their native language. Then, as an older child, she was adopted by an immigrant Hungarian family. "The saying goes that the stories grew out of that family like hair grows out of people's heads," she says of her adoptive family.

In rural Michigan, where she grew up, "I was surrounded by poor immigrants," Pinkola Estés says, "people who had come from all over because there was work for those who did not read

1. **psychologist** (seye-KAHL-uh-jihst) *n.* one who studies the mind and behavior
2. **phenomenon** (fih-NAH-muh-nahn) *n.* an unusual fact or occurrence
3. **migrant workers** (MEYE-gruhnt) *n. pl.* people who move from place to place picking crops

or write." There were mountain people from Kentucky, Eastern Europeans, Mexicans, and African Americans. And every group, she recalls, "brought their music and their tales."

When she was 6 years old, she understood why stories were so important to her adoptive parents. Like her birth parents, the Pinkolas could not read or write. "Before I learned to write, I made poems, rhyming ones so I could remember them," she says. "I remember in exquisite[4] detail my amazement to find that there were little black curls and lines you could make on paper that you could then read."

Once she could read, "the greatest longing of my young life was for books to read and paper to write on. A university student from the next county over was sweet on me—I was about 14. He brought over a packet of books, wondering if I would like to read them." Her father would not let her go out with the student, Pinkola Estés says. "The boy went away, and I have often silently blessed him and the fate that drew him to me just to give me these precious[5] books." The student's gift "is how, in this cornfield in the middle of nowhere, where girls grew up to be grandmothers or else gang members, I became related to living poets and their work."

After high school, Pinkola Estés began traveling. Everywhere she went, she listened to folktales and fairy tales with morals about such common subjects as what happens to children who don't tell the truth. She learned how different cultures use stories to pass on knowledge and to reinforce cultural values. Along the way, she was married, divorced, and found herself in her 20s with a young family to support. "I would get up at 5 A.M. and go bake bread to get money for my children," she says. "There wasn't anything else I could do. But all the time, I was planning my escape."

Part of that escape was writing. "I discovered 25 years ago that, if I kept at it, I could write about two-and-a-half pages in

---

4. **exquisite** (ehk-SKWIH-zuht) *adj.* carefully done; precise
5. **precious** (PREH-shuhs) *adj.* of great value

five or six minutes. Every time I had a little space of time, I read or wrote." She wrote stories and poetry, and she wrote about the questions people ask about life.

When she was in her 30s, she traveled to Mexico to meet her birth family. They "not only embraced me but recognized my poetic spirit," she says. Pinkola Estés already regarded herself as a *cantadora* (kahn-tah-DOHR-ah), or Mexican storyteller. The visits she began making regularly to Mexico enriched[6] her stories. She also began to study people who were different, "or who are pushed out of the mainstream in one way or another. What I found out—and I love this—was that most useful things ever invented came from so-called exiles."[7]

Pinkola Estés settled in Denver, Colorado, and went to Loretto Heights College. She graduated in 1976, then earned her Ph.D. in multicultural psychology from the Union Institute in Cincinnati, Ohio. Her study focused on cultural groups. In 1984, she earned a diploma in Jungian analysis.[8] Jungian analysis is based on the work of Carl Jung, a Swiss doctor. He believed that all people, regardless of their culture, have the same images in their minds. These images relate to common experiences such as finding a mate and having children. They also appear in religion. Jung thought that symbols can help people understand themselves better.

Pinkola Estés returned to Denver and became a practicing psychoanalyst and the head of the C. G. Jung Center for Education and Research in Denver. She also co-founded a shelter for battered women in Colorado and taught writing to men and women in prisons.

During this time, she never stopped writing. Every few years she would send her writing to publishers. They would send back rejection[9] letters. "Eventually, I had a 2,500-page work about the

---

6. **enriched** (ihn-RIHCHT) *v.* made more valuable

7. **exiles** (EHG-zeyelz) *n. pl.* people who are forced to leave their homeland; those who do not fit into a community or culture

8. **analysis** (uh-NA-luh-suhs) *n.* the study of a person's mind

9. **rejection** (rih-JEHK-shuhn) *adj.* refusing; not accepting of something

inner life," she says. "I thought I'd be done by the time I was 30, and then 35, and then 40," she says. "Actually, nothing happened until the year I turned 45."

That year, she met her current husband. "I had not thought that love would come this late," she says. He was a master sergeant in the Air Force. He loved her writing and that led to their marriage. Then, in 1989, she went on a Boulder radio station to talk about Jung. "Someone else was supposed to go," she says, "but they got sick, so I went instead."

The woman who interviewed Pinkola Estés was Tami Simon, who is president of Sounds True, a company that makes and sells audiotapes.[10] Simon thought that a tape on Jungian analysis might sell well, and she liked the way Pinkola Estés had handled the interview. Pinkola Estés "came up with 50 ideas," of what she could tape, Simon recalls, "but I had no idea if she could pull it off."

Pinkola Estés came to the studio and taped her stories. The first tapes, called *Journey Into Creativity,* explain how people can become more creative. Pinkola Estés recorded a new tape every few months. Soon they were the most popular tapes Sounds True sold. "We have a file of 200 letters about how these tapes have affected people," Simon says. "We've sold upwards of 30,000."

Publishers who had heard of the storytelling tapes asked how they could get in touch with Pinkola Estés. They called her. They wrote to her. Confused and overwhelmed, Pinkola Estés talked to an agent. Soon six publishers were in a bidding war for her book.

Once a publisher had signed on, Pinkola Estés had to trim the thousands of pages she had written into a book. "I was writing and polishing 17 hours a day, seven days per week for six months," she says. The resulting book features 19 folk- and fairy tales that can help people, particularly women, understand themselves by finding themselves in the stories. One chapter, for instance, focuses on the fairy tale of the little match girl who is

---

10. **audiotapes** (AWD-ee-oh-tayps) *n. pl.* sound recordings

outdoors on a freezing night. She sees wonderful fantasies when she lights the matches, but freezes to death. The point, Pinkola Estés says, is that the girl is living on fantasies, not action. If the girl paid attention to what she really wanted to do, she would know better than to waste the matches, which represent her fire, or her creative energy. The title of the book refers to the inner self that she feels is free and wise like a wolf.

Pinkola Estés is now working on a second book. She still tells stories as a *cantadora*. "I hope you will go out and let stories happen to you," she writes in *Women Who Run with the Wolves*. When these stories happen, Pinkola Estés believes, people will discover how to fully live their lives.

> ***Did You Know?*** *Mexican migrant workers have been a part of U.S. farm life for most of this century. They travel to harvest crops as they ripen. Some migrants have come from Mexico to pick crops in this country. Others have been Mexican Americans. In the 1960s, César Chávez, a Mexican American, was angry about the way migrant workers were treated. He formed the National Farm Workers Association. The Farm Workers today continue to work to improve the often poor conditions under which migrants work. They talk to the farmers to get better contracts for migrant workers and they lobby for better regulation of pesticides.*

AFTER YOU READ

EXPLORING YOUR RESPONSES

1. Pinkola Estés talks about places in her childhood that were important to her. Why might a place be important to a child?

2. Books were important to Pinkola Estés when she was young, and still are. Tell about a book you have enjoyed.

3. Pinkola Estés tried again and again to sell her writing, but no one would publish it. How might you avoid giving up if you were in that situation?

4. Pinkola Estés's parents could not read or write. How do you think your life would be different if you could not read or write?

5. Retell a fairy tale or folktale that has a moral.

UNDERSTANDING WORDS IN CONTEXT

Read the following sentences from the biography. Think about what each underlined word means. In your notebook, write what the word means as it is used in the sentence.

1. Pinkola Estés is a celebrity who receives hundreds of letters a week and who gets mobbed when she arrives at readings. She is a publishing phenomenon.

2. "I remember in exquisite detail my amazement to find that there were little black curls and lines you could make on paper that you could then read."

3. "The boy went away, and I have often silently blessed him and the fate that drew him to me just to give me these precious books."

4. She also began to study people who were different, or who are pushed out of the mainstream in one way or another.

"What I found out—and I love this—was that most useful things ever invented came from so-called exiles."

5. Every few years she would send her writing to publishers. They would send back rejection letters.

RECALLING DETAILS

1. Why did poor immigrants come to rural Michigan?

2. How did Pinkola Estés get the paper and books she wanted when she was young?

3. Describe Jung's ideas about symbols.

4. How did Pinkola Estés gain acceptance by the public?

5. How did *Women Who Run With the Wolves* become a best seller?

UNDERSTANDING INFERENCES

In your notebook, write two or three sentences from the biography that support each of the following inferences.

1. Many people who read Pinkola Estés's book think it contains important advice.

2. Pinkola Estés has an affection and an interest in people who don't fit into society.

3. Pinkola Estés's adoptive parents and birth parents had some similar characteristics.

4. Being raised with people from many cultures helped shape Pinkola Estés's work.

5. The publishing world did not think *Women Who Run With the Wolves* would be a best seller.

INTERPRETING WHAT YOU HAVE READ

1. What early evidence was there that Pinkola Estés had a literary interest?

2. How did having roots in both the Hungarian and Mexican cultures affect Pinkola Estés?

3. Why do you think that inventions might often come from people who do not feel part of the mainstream?

4. Why do you think Pinkola Estés decided to study Jungian analysis?

5. Why did Pinkola Estés keep writing even after publishers kept rejecting her work?

ANALYZING QUOTATIONS

Read the following quotation from the biography and answer the questions below.

> *"What I found out—and I love this—was that most useful things ever invented came from so-called exiles."*

1. Who are the "so-called exiles" in this quotation?

2. Why do you think Pinkola Estés loved the idea that exiles invented useful things?

3. Do you agree with Pinkola Estés? Explain your response.

THINKING CRITICALLY

1. Why do you think *Women Who Run With the Wolves* has become so popular?

2. Why do you think so many cultures tell fairy tales and folktales?

3. How is listening to audiotapes of a story different from reading the book?

4. Do you think Pinkola Estés would have found a publisher if the tapes had not been successful? Explain your answer.

5. Pinkola Estés did not have much encouragement to keep writing, but she did. How can encouragement affect a person's work?

ADRIANA OCAMPO

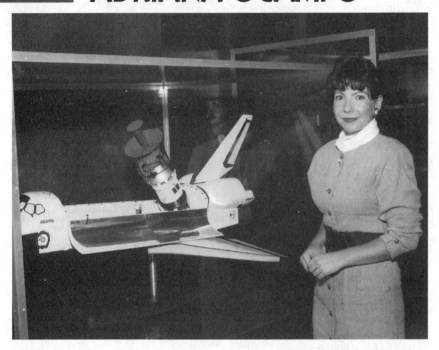

Adriana Ocampo, a planetary geologist with NASA, stands next to the *Galileo* spacecraft. A native of Colombia, Ocampo was the science coordinator of the Near Infrared Mapping Spectrometer (N.I.M.S.), one of the instruments used in the *Galileo*.

Adriana Ocampo (oh-KAHM-poh) dreamed of creating colonies on other worlds. As a small girl she designed them on paper, waking up her parents to show them her latest marvels. "Instead of playing with dolls like other little girls, Adriana was making astronauts out of them," her mother, Teresa Uria Ocampo, says. Today, instead of using kitchen appliances to build spacecraft, she designs instruments that travel in outer space to study Jupiter.

Ocampo was born in Barranquilla (bahrr-ahn-KEE-yah), Colombia in 1955, but when she was a baby her family moved to Buenos Aires, Argentina. Her mother was a preschool teacher, her father a Navy chief technician who spent most of his career in electronics. "There was plenty of time to play and explore," Ocampo says. "We lived close to nature. There were a lot of farms nearby."

When she was still a small child, her parents bought her a book about planets and space travel. "They knew I was always intrigued with space," she says. "From that point, I wanted to explore space, to be an astronaut." It was a difficult path to follow in Argentina, though. The country had no space program.

When Ocampo was in junior high, she was tested to find out which career she should pursue.[1] Argentina's schooling is "very strict," Ocampo says. "You only get to select a few of your subjects." The test said Ocampo should be an accountant.[2] Her parents sent her to a high school that prepared students to do just that. "I hated it," Ocampo says.

Ocampo was 16 years old when her parents, who were "looking for new horizons" and worried about what they

---

1. **pursue** (puhr-SOO) *v.* to follow
2. **accountant** (uh-KOWN-tuhnt) *n.* someone who keeps track of the money spent and received by a person or business

considered to be the unstable[3] political situation in Argentina, decided to move to the United States. (See **Did You Know?** on page 158 for more information about Argentina's political history.) "My father had been to a Harvard program on a scholarship and he loved the U.S.," Ocampo says. Her father found work as an electrician in Los Angeles in 1969. The next year, the rest of the family joined him in the United States.

"I was tremendously excited," Ocampo recalls. The United States, after all, had sent a man to the moon. Ocampo's father settled them in a neighborhood with a large Latino population. He didn't know that the neighborhood also had problems with gang warfare. "It was a big change. I had a kid pull a knife on me. I was so amazed by it," she says. "We moved to South Pasadena as soon as we could afford to."

Ocampo, whose ancestors[4] came from Spain, spoke no English when she came to the United States. In high school, she had studied French. Soon, however, she learned the language and the customs of the United States. High school in Argentina was more difficult, Ocampo says, which helped make the change to a new school and a new language easier. One of the things she had to learn was that the attitude toward teachers was different here. "We had high respect for the teacher in Argentina. You stood up every time the teacher came in. So here, when the teacher came in, I stood up. The other students were saying, 'What is she doing?' "

Ocampo's introduction to different races came in this country, too. The great mix of people in California is "one of the greatest aspects"[5] of the state, Ocampo says. "People do things all different ways. It's very enriching."

Even with the desire to fit into a new country, Ocampo never forgot her passion for space. When the Explorers, a scouting group, came to her high school looking for new members who

---

3. **unstable** (uhn-STAY-buhl) *adj.* changing rapidly; uncertain
4. **ancestors** (AN-sehs-tuhrz) *n. pl.* people from whom a person is descended
5. **aspects** (AS-pehkts) *n. pl.* features; the ways that something looks

wanted to learn about space exploration, Ocampo eagerly joined. "That was a fantastic program," she remembers.

The club had help from scientists who worked at the Jet Propulsion Laboratory (JPL), part of the National Aeronautics and Space Administration (NASA). There were also summer internships at the lab. Ocampo went to work there after her junior year in high school. She hasn't left. The summer job turned into a part-time job during the school year. Ocampo began college at Pasadena City College, and later went to California State University in Los Angeles.

While working at the lab, Ocampo says, "a scientist from the *Viking* Project that went to Mars asked if I'd be interested in working on that." Ocampo became involved in a mission that included taking pictures of the moons of Mars. "That's when planetary geology was really taking off," Ocampo explains. Planetary geology is just what it sounds like—the study of the physical makeup[6] of other planets. Since it's impossible right now to get actual samples of distant planets, scientists have to create new ways to obtain the information they need. "It's a great challenge to develop the techniques."[7] Ocampo's most thrilling moment as a planetary geologist came in 1976 when *Viking* landed on Mars. She helped produce the only atlas of two of Mars' moons, Phobos and Deimos.

In 1993, the *Mars Observer*, on which Ocampo worked for years, was lost. "It was very painful," Ocampo says. "It's not only the science questions we were going to try to answer. It was the people you work with, the team. They become your family." When the *Observer* was lost, "It was almost like somebody died. It really felt like that."

Among other projects, Ocampo is now working on the *Hermes* (HUR-meez) mission to explore the planet Mercury. Ocampo is also trying to bring together North and South America to talk about space. "Knowledge isn't worth very much

---

6. **makeup** (MAY-kuhp) *n.* the way in which the parts of something are put together; its composition
7. **techniques** (tehk-NEEKS) *n. pl.* methods of bringing about a result

if only the few have it," she says. She organized a conference to share information in 1990 in Costa Rica, and in 1993 a second conference was held in Chile.

Ocampo has one offbeat[8] but fascinating discovery to her credit. She was the first to recognize that a ring of sinkholes in the Yucatán Peninsula in Mexico was the result of an enormous meteorite[9] that smashed into Earth 65 million years ago. That impact may well have been a major reason the Earth's atmosphere changed, causing the dinosaurs to become extinct. Ocampo believes that the impact of the crash created dust and gases that caused acid rain, decreasing the dinosaurs' food supply.

Her profession, with its far-reaching goals, has made her into someone with global interests, she says. "I think of myself as a planetary citizen. It's part of the science, that you have to look at things globally."

> **Did You Know?** *By 1970, when the Ocampo family immigrated to the United States from Argentina, Argentina was in the grip of political chaos. In 1955, dictator Juan Perón had been driven from power by the military after he failed to create prosperity. However, his followers continued to plot for his return, weakening the power of the military government. The resulting economic uncertainty caused many Argentines to leave their country.*

---

8. **offbeat** (awf-BEET) *adj.* unusual; odd
9. **meteorite** (MEE-tee-uh-reyet) *n.* a piece of matter from space that lands on Earth

AFTER YOU READ

EXPLORING YOUR RESPONSES

1. What interests did you have as a child that you still enjoy?

2. Do you think that people should decide on a career early in life or wait until after high school?

3. Schools in Argentina are very different from those in the United States. What is your idea of a perfect school?

4. When she was working on the *Mars Observer* project, Ocampo worked closely with a group of other scientists. What are the positives and negatives to working with a group?

5. Ocampo joined a club at school that led to her job at NASA. Think of a career that interests you. How could you start preparing yourself for that career?

UNDERSTANDING WORDS IN CONTEXT

Read the following sentences from the biography. Think about what each underlined word means. In your notebook, write what the word means as it is used in the sentence.

1. When Ocampo was in junior high, she was tested to find out which career she should pursue.

2. Ocampo was 16 years old when her parents, who were "looking for new horizons" and worried about what they considered to be the unstable political situation in Argentina, decided to move to the United States.

3. Planetary geology is just what it sounds like—the study of the physical makeup of other planets.

4. Scientists have to create new ways to obtain the information they need. "It's a great challenge to develop the techniques."

5. She was the first to recognize that a ring of sinkholes in the Yucatán Peninsula in Mexico was the result of an enormous meteorite that smashed into Earth 65 million years ago.

RECALLING DETAILS

1. What was the first sign that Ocampo was interested in studying space?

2. Why did Ocampo's family move to the United States?

3. Name three of the differences Ocampo noticed between life in Argentina and life in the United States.

4. Name two of Ocampo's professional accomplishments.

5. Why did Ocampo organize a conference on space for countries in the Americas?

UNDERSTANDING INFERENCES

In your notebook, write two or three sentences from the biography that support each of the following inferences.

1. Ocampo's life in Argentina was more sheltered than her life in Los Angeles was.

2. In Argentina, people believe high school students should not be given much independence.

3. Working intensely on a project creates close bonds between people.

4. Planetary geology can lead to discoveries on Earth.

5. Ocampo's view of the world has been influenced by her career.

INTERPRETING WHAT YOU HAVE READ

1. How did Ocampo's parents help support their daughter's interest in space?

2. What do you think was the biggest problem Ocampo faced as an immigrant to the United States?

3. Do you think the study of planetary geology is useful to us on Earth? Explain your answer.

4. What do you think Ocampo enjoys about her job?

5. How does Ocampo's heritage affect her work?

ANALYZING QUOTATIONS

Read the following quotation from the biography and answer the questions below.

"I think of myself as a planetary citizen. It's part of the science, that you have to look at things globally."

1. What does it mean to be a "planetary citizen"?

2. How could feeling like a planetary citizen change a person's behavior?

3. Do you think of yourself more as a U.S. citizen or a planetary citizen? Why?

THINKING CRITICALLY

1. How does your high school differ from Ocampo's high school in Argentina?

2. How might Ocampo's life have been different if she had stayed in Argentina?

3. Name two ways that conferences like the ones Ocampo organized in Costa Rica and Chile can help scientists learn more about the earth and about space.

4. Ocampo says she looks at things globally. What evidence do we have that this is true?

5. What aspect of Ocampo's job interests you most? Why?

CULTURAL CONNECTIONS

Thinking About What People Do

1. Success in science or mathematics usually requires a great deal of time spent in field research. Describe the research activities of two of the people in this unit.

2. Imagine that you had to introduce one person from this unit to your family or class. Write a short statement of introduction so your audience will know about some of that person's achievements. Present your introduction to the class.

3. The people in this unit have made many contributions to the sciences and mathematics. Discuss how the work of one of them has affected your life or is likely to affect it in the future.

4. Imagine that you are one of the people in this unit. Write an entry in your diary about an important discovery you have just made. Describe your work and share your feelings about your achievement.

Thinking About Culture

1. Role models can play an important part in a person's life. Choose two subjects from this unit and discuss how they were influenced by others early in their lives.

2. Most of the biographies in this unit tell about the subjects' leaving their homeland. Compare two of the subjects and give their reasons for emigrating to the United States.

3. Choose one person from this unit and explain how his or her work is important to countries throughout the world. Give examples of how he or she is a global citizen.

Building Research Skills

Work with a partner to complete the following activity.

The families of the five people you have read about in this unit were born in five different Latin American locations. Select one of these places and make notes of some facts you would like to learn about it. Include questions such as the following:

☆ How do the people in this location make a living—through manufacturing, farming, tourism, or other means?

Hint: The Bibliography at the back of this book will give you a list of books and articles that can help you begin your research.

☆ How has its geographic location influenced its development?

☆ What form of government exists today?

☆ What forms of entertainment are most popular: music, dance, theater, movies, TV, or a combination of these?

Hint: Use the subject index of the card catalog or computer data base to locate nonfiction books and articles from such magazines as National Geographic for your investigation. Look also for recordings or videos.

☆ What school or community activities do most teenagers enjoy?

Next, go to the library to find the answers to your questions.

Prepare a poster in the form of an oversized encyclopedia entry. Organize your information by topic, such as environment, people, geography, or culture. Prepare headlines as well as illustrations drawn or copied from your reference sources. You might also add objects, souvenirs, artifacts, or travel brochures from the region. Include a list of the materials you used for your research.

Present your finished display to your classmates or to another class. Be prepared to answer questions or direct students to your sources for further investigation.

Extending Your Studies

HEALTH **Your task:** *To write a public relations campaign for a health agency.* You read in this unit about former Surgeon General Antonia Novello's work in warning young Americans about the dangers of smoking, drinking, and AIDS. Choose one of these health problems for further investigation. Look in your library for pamphlets or other educational materials published by local or national organizations that target this subject. Write to these organizations for more information or visit a branch office in your community. With your classmates, design informational posters and flyers. Try to convey the importance of your message by using direct, simple slogans and bright colors.

Your campaign might include:

☆ slogans   ☆ a mascot

☆ posters   ☆ T-shirt designs

☆ flyers   ☆ fact sheets or bookmarks

☆ stickers   ☆ jingles or songs

Plan your public relations campaign, and present it at a school Health Day assembly.

SOCIAL STUDIES/ SCIENCE **Your task:** *To draw up an action plan for saving the rain forests.* As you read in this unit, Francisco Dallmeier studies what is happening to rain forests around the world and is trying to find ways to stop the destruction. Work with a small group to find out more about rain forests. Use newspapers, magazines, and other reference materials from your library. These questions might help you begin:

☆ Which areas of the world are covered by rain forests?

☆ Why are rain forests being cut down?

☆ What plants and animals would be endangered if rain forests were destroyed?

Organize your information about rain forests with your group members. Use a world map or atlas to focus on the scope of the issue. Then brainstorm ways that individual students can make a difference with this global problem. Write a list of actions that would protect rain forests. Which items could be carried out in your school? In your community? Make plans with your group to carry out one or more items on your action plan. Write a news item for the school newspaper that describes your progress.

MATHEMATICS **Your task:** *To prepare a brief oral report on a topic in mathematics.* Concepts in mathematics are mentioned throughout this unit. Look back to find these in the text:

☆ Jaime Escalante: calculus
Mayan concept of zero

☆ Francisco Dallmeier: exploding population in Latin America

☆ Antonia Novello: smoking among adults
health insurance

☆ Adriana Ocampo profession of accounting

Choose one of these mathematics topics that interests you. Work with a group to investigate your topic. Use materials in your classroom, your school, or a local library, or interview teachers or family members. Write an outline of what you learned, including definitions of terms, statistics, and other data. Prepare a short oral presentation for the class and illustrate your talk, if possible, using overhead transparencies or charts.

WRITING WORKSHOP

In Unit 2, you wrote a biographical sketch of a friend. You portrayed that friend through an experience you shared. The details you used came from your, or your friend's, memory. For this activity, you will write a **biographical sketch of someone in your family or community**. You will gather your information by conducting an interview.

PREWRITING

Get started with these **prewriting** steps:

Select a subject: Think about the people in your family—not only those who live with you but other relatives as well. Ask your family for their suggestions. You might also write about someone in your community—perhaps someone who has done or achieved something special. In your notebook, jot down three or four names and some information about each person. Then select the person who most interests you, who you think will interest others, and about whom you can gather information.

Gather information: After you select your subject, collect facts and ideas about the person and write them in a notebook. In addition to what you may know or can find out from others, you can research other sources, such as community calendars or newsletters, personal letters, and newspaper and magazine articles. Record your findings in your notebook.

Arrange an interview: Set up an interview with your subject or someone who knows that person well.

Organize your questions: Read through the material in your notebook and write questions you will ask during the interview. When you look over your facts, you may find some gaps in your information. These should be the basis for some of your questions. Here are a few ideas to help you begin:

☆ What was your childhood like?

☆ What kinds of recreation or entertainment do you enjoy?

☆ What work do you do?

☆ Who are your heroes?

☆ Of which achievements are you particularly proud?

☆ What are your goals?

Arrange your questions in the order in which you plan to use them. Arrange the facts you already know nearby. Leave room in your notebook for the subject's answers. In the interview, you may find that the answer to one question leads you to ask a new, unplanned question. Don't be afraid to go in a new direction. Prepare more questions than you need, in case things do not go exactly as you planned.

Conduct the interview: Be polite and efficient during your interview. Avoid questions that can be answered with "yes" or "no." Take notes or record your subject's answers, first asking for permission to do so. Thank the subject when the interview is complete.

Organize your notes: As soon after the interview as possible, go over your notes and organize them. Use chronological, or time, order, if this works best for your material. Since you cannot include every detail you've uncovered, decide on a main idea or event as the focus of your biographical sketch. Narrow your focus by asking: What is the one thing I want my readers to learn about my subject? For example:

Subject: Paul, the new lifeguard at Harmon Beach

Focus: How I helped him rescue a young boy last summer

What I learned: Staying alert can pay off and help others

DRAFTING

Once you have organized your notes and decided on a main idea, you can start **drafting** your biographical sketch. Your opening sentence should make the reader curious about your subject. For example:

> *How could I have known that my love of ice cream on a hot summer day could help the lifeguard save Jimmy Sanders from drowning?*

Use details and descriptions in the body of the biography to build a clear portrait of your subject in the reader's mind.

By the end of your biographical sketch, your reader should "know" your subject and understand what he or she has learned from the event. For example:

> *Don't forget to be alert whenever you are at the ocean. You never know when you'll be part of a daring rescue!*

REVISING

Put your biographical sketch aside for a day or two. Then, with the help of another student who will act as your editor, evaluate and **revise** your work. See the directions for writers and student editors below.

Directions for Writers: Before you give your writing to a student editor, read your work aloud to hear how it sounds. Then ask yourself the following questions:

☆ Does my opening hold the reader's attention?

☆ Am I *showing*, not *telling*, the reader what happened?

☆ Did I use colorful details?

☆ Does my description make my subject come alive?

☆ Does my ending sum up the biography's focus?

Make notes for your next draft or revise your writing before you give it to your student editor. Then ask your student editor to read your sketch. Listen carefully to his or her suggestions. If they seem helpful, use them to improve your writing when you revise your work.

Directions for Student Editors: Read the work carefully and respectfully, keeping in mind that your purpose is to help the writer do his or her best work. Remember that an editor should always make positive, helpful comments that point to specific parts of the essay. After you read the work, use the following questions to help you direct your comments:

☆ What do I like most about the biographical sketch?

☆ What would I like to know more about?

☆ Can I picture the scene or event in my mind?

☆ Do I feel I know the subject?

PROOFREADING

When you are satisfied that your work says what you want it to say, **proofread** it for errors in spelling, punctuation, capitalization, and grammar. Then make a neat, final copy of your biographical sketch.

PUBLISHING

After you have revised and proofread your work, you are ready to **publish** it. Make a cover for your sketch and illustrate it with something that complements the subject. Perhaps you can find or take a photograph of your subject. Arrange the title and the illustration in an attractive design that will grab the attention of your readers and say something about your subject. Share your biographical sketch with your classmates in a Who's Who display or presentation.

UNIT 4

LATINOS IN PUBLIC SERVICE AND BUSINESS

In this unit, you will read about six Latinos who have achieved success in public service or business. What events and challenges did each of them experience that inspired them to reach their goals? As you read the selections, think about how each person's cultural background has helped them succeed.

"Imagine a Great City," said **Federico Peña** (PEHN-yah) to Denver voters in his winning campaign for mayor in 1982. Then, in 1993, President Clinton named this young Mexican American lawyer to be U.S. Secretary of Transportation.

Ileana Ros-Lehtinen (rohs LEH-teh-nen) speaks strongly for her native Cuba in her position as United States Representative from Florida. She challenges all Latinas to "re-energize . . . to realize [our] vast potential."

Strength from her parents helped Mexican American **Linda Alvarado** (ahl-vah-RAH-doh) face discrimination: "Self-confidence was the greatest gift they gave us." Today Alvarado owns a construction company and a major-league baseball team.

Cuban-born **Roberto Goizueta** (goi-SWEH-tah) believes that businesses must not focus on just one country. He has remade his company, Coca-Cola, so that "Now we are a large international company with a sizable American business."

Fashion and perfume designer **Oscar de la Renta** (day lah REN-tah) supports needy children in his homeland: "There is no way you can escape it. [The Dominican Republic] is such a small country that one voice makes a difference."

Lawyer **Antonia Hernández** (er-NAHN-des) seeks social justice for her fellow Mexican Americans: "My parents instilled in us the belief that serving the public interest was a very noble thing to do."

As you read these biographies, think about how these people have worked to solve problems in the world.

FEDERICO PEÑA

U.S. Transportation Secretary Federico Peña (right) surveys the damage to the 118 Freeway from the February, 1994, earthquake in Northridge, California. Pictured with Peña are the winner of the contract to rebuild the roadway, Leonard Brutoco (center), and the administrator of federal highways, Rodney Slater (left). Peña, who is Mexican American, has found that persistence has helped him achieve his goals.

They came pushing through the door, thousands of them, smiling, crying, hugging. When they saw Federico Peña (PEHN-ya), the crowd exploded in a deafening roar. "We have set history in this country tonight!" Peña shouted, raising his arms high. "All the rules in politics have been broken!"

Peña was right. When he began his campaign for mayor of Denver in 1982, less than 3 percent of the population even knew who Peña was. He was also only 36 years old. If elected, he would be one of the youngest mayors in the country. But most damaging of all, political experts thought, was that Peña was Latino. How could he be elected in a city that had a Latino population of only 18 percent? He was a hopeless dreamer, the experts decided.

As his opponents have learned, it is a mistake to underestimate Federico Peña. Once he decided he wanted to become mayor of Denver, he worked tirelessly. People began to see the young candidate everywhere, talking earnestly with whomever would listen. Soon he had an astonishing 4,000 volunteers. His slogan, "Imagine a Great City," captured Denver's imagination. This candidate had dreams for Denver, big dreams. He wanted a new airport, a new convention center, a baseball team.

The experts were stunned when Peña came in first in a field of seven candidates in the election in May 1983. But Peña still faced a runoff election—no one had enough votes to win the election outright.

In the month between the first election and the runoff, something remarkable happened. People who had never even thought of voting began to register to vote. Many were Latino and had thought that their votes meant nothing. By the cutoff date, more than 6,000 new voters registered, some answering simply "Peña" when asked their political party.

The month between elections gave Peña's challenger a chance to use racial fears. He mailed questionnaires to voters asking them whether it mattered that Peña was Latino.

Apparently it didn't. Peña's new ideas and energy appealed to a majority of Denver's voters. But after Peña won the election, reality set in. People wanted action—now. They had elected him for change. Unfortunately, just as Peña began working on his ambitious[1] plans, trouble hit. Denver's economy went straight downward as the oil boom that had fueled much of the city's growth faded. Also, because Peña prefers to act only after considerable thought, people who were losing their jobs became angry at what they saw as endless planning.

When Peña ran for reelection in 1987, he was expected to lose. Once again, the experts were wrong. When the bitter campaign was over, Peña had won, 51 to 49 percent.

One advantage Peña had through these painful campaigns was charisma[2] and a political know-how that almost seems to be inherited. His family has been in public life in Texas for two centuries. One ancestor was mayor of Laredo during the Civil War. (See **Did You Know?** on page 177 for more information about the Mexican heritage of Texas.)

Federico Peña was born in 1947 in Laredo and grew up in Brownsville, Texas, as the third of six children in a middle-class home. His father, Gustavo Peña, is a cotton broker who arranged deals between local growers and buyers. "We had people from England, from Japan, from France come over for dinner," Peña remembers.

At home the family spoke both English and Spanish, as many families in Brownsville did. The town's population was about 85 percent Latino, and there was little discrimination.

His upbringing was strict. Peña and his brothers and sisters were expected to obey their parents without question and to help earn money for college. By the time Peña went to college at the University of Texas in Austin, he had worked in jobs ranging from pouring concrete to working in a sorghum[3] plant.

---

1. **ambitious** (am-BIH-shuhs) *adj.* wanting to reach a goal; challenging
2. **charisma** (kuh-RIHZ-muh) *n.* magnetic appeal; charm
3. **sorghum** (SAWR-guhm) *n.* a plant used to make sugar syrup

Attending college at the largely white, wealthy University of Texas took a major adjustment. "There were no minorities on campus," Peña recalls. For the first time, "I ran into clear discrimination. There were people who wouldn't talk to me."

It didn't take long for Peña to shake off his bewilderment[4] and make friends. When he was a senior, he ran as Mickey Mouse in a mock campaign for student body president to show how cartoonish the position was. He even wore a Mickey Mouse costume to underscore his point. He came in second.

Also when he was a senior in college, Peña decided to become a lawyer. There was one problem, however. "I do not test well, but I make up for it with hard work." When his scores for the test to enter law school were low, Peña was persistent.[5] "I kept bugging the dean, and he finally let me in," Peña remembers.

After law school graduation, Peña visited his brother Alfredo in Denver, fell in love with the city, and moved there. He began working as a lawyer for MALDEF, the Mexican American Legal Defense and Education Fund, as an activist lawyer. (For more information about MALDEF, see the biography of MALDEF president Antonia Hernández on page 217.) He handled civil rights cases, worked on police brutality cases, and tried to expand voting rights for Latinos.

That urge to make a difference led Peña to run for the state legislature in 1978, at the age of 31. Not only did he win the election, but he was also reelected, elected Democratic leader of the House, and voted outstanding legislator of the year in 1981.

Despite this success, Peña was frustrated with his inability to get things going. In 1982, he ran for mayor. Peña began to put his carefully thought-out plans for the new airport and the convention center into action. Before he could get started, though, he faced one of the biggest challenges of his career—an effort to recall[6] him from office. The recall attempt was begun

---

4. **bewilderment** (bih-WIHL-duhr-muhnt) *n.* the feeling of being confused or puzzled
5. **persistent** (puhr-SIHS-tuhnt) *adj.* determined; insistent
6. **recall** (rih-KAWL) *v.* to remove an elected official by a vote of the people

by former city employees who had been fired and by citizens who were frustrated by all the plans that had not yet been translated into action. Others were angry because a late-season snowstorm had snarled traffic for weeks.

The recall effort failed, and by the end of his second term, Peña accomplished almost everything he told voters he would do. Citizens voted to approve construction of a huge new airport that opened in 1994. Peña built the convention center and played a central role in bringing major league baseball to Denver. By sticking to his plan despite the storms that surrounded him, stubborn Federico Peña delivered. He also married Ellen Hart, a former world-class distance runner he had met at a race. They now have two daughters.

In 1991, with his popularity rising, he shocked the same political experts who predicted that he would never be elected. He decided not to run for a third term. Peña believes that officials shouldn't stay too long in public jobs. Instead, he started a Latino-owned investment firm.

It didn't take long for newly elected President Bill Clinton to come calling. He asked Peña to run the transition for the Department of Transportation, which employs about 11,000 people and has an annual budget of over $4 billion. Then Clinton surprised political Washington and offered Peña the job of Secretary of Transportation. The answer was yes.

Peña faces a serious set of problems, from crumbling roads to unprofitable airlines to the constant infighting that is common in Washington. Fewer people count Federico Peña out now. "People meet me and they think I'm a nice guy, a pushover," Peña says. "They find out the one way to get me fired up is to come at me."

He proved his value to the President during the January 1994 earthquake that rocked Los Angeles. Peña was the first on the scene, and he rolled up his sleeves and got to work. He approved a federal contract to remove crumpled concrete. He urged commuters fed up with the jammed freeways to use public transit. His down-to-earth style impressed California. U.S. Sen.

Dianne Feinstein told him, "If I had to rank you on a scale of one to ten, I would give you a ten on this disaster."

For Peña, who was already on to the next crisis, it was confirmation[7] that hard work and persistence bring results.

> **Did You Know?** *Although Anglos had been moving into what is now Texas for decades, the land was still considered part of Mexico until 1845. In that year, the U.S. House of Representatives made Texas a state, and the Mexicans who decided to stay there became the first Mexican Americans. The annexation of Texas was the reason for the Mexican War, which lasted from 1846-1848. The United States won and Mexico gave up nearly half its territory, including what became California, Nevada, Utah, New Mexico, Colorado, Wyoming, and parts of Arizona. The Mexicans in those areas were given the choice of becoming U.S. citizens or returning to Mexico. About 80 percent decided to stay and become citizens.*

---

7. **confirmation** (kahn-fuhr-MAY-shuhn) *n.* proof; evidence

AFTER YOU READ

EXPLORING YOUR RESPONSES

1. When Federico Peña decided he wanted to become mayor, he worked day and night. What might you work that hard for?

2. How would you advise someone to respond who had been a victim of prejudice?

3. When he was growing up, Peña met people from many different countries. What country are you most interested in learning about? Why?

4. If you were mayor of your town, what problem would you most want to solve? How might you solve it?

5. When Peña meets resistance, he becomes stubborn and works harder. What other strategies could a person use to succeed?

UNDERSTANDING WORDS IN CONTEXT

Read the following sentences from the biography. Think about what each underlined word means. In your notebook, write what the word means as it is used in the sentence.

1. People wanted action—now. They had elected him for change. Unfortunately, just as Peña began working on his ambitious plans, trouble hit.

2. One advantage Peña had through these painful campaigns was charisma and a political know-how that almost seems to be inherited.

3. "There were people who wouldn't talk to me." It didn't take long for Peña to shake off his bewilderment and use his natural ability to make friends.

4. When his scores for the test to enter law school were low, Peña was persistent. "I kept bugging the dean, and he finally let me in," Peña remembers.

5. "If I had to rank you on a scale of one to ten, I would give you a ten on this disaster." For Peña, who was already on to the next crisis, it was <u>confirmation</u> that hard work and persistence bring results.

RECALLING DETAILS

1. Why did some people think that Peña would not be elected mayor of Denver?

2. Why did Latinos sign up to vote just before Denver's mayoral runoff election?

3. Why did Peña find college a major adjustment?

4. What were some of Peña's accomplishments in Denver?

5. Why did voters try to recall Peña from office?

UNDERSTANDING INFERENCES

In your notebook, write two or three sentences that support each of the following inferences.

1. Politics had interested Peña long before he ran for mayor of Denver.

2. Peña has worked for justice for Latinos.

3. Peña's determination has helped him become successful.

4. Peña enjoys being faced with challenges.

5. Peña's experience as mayor has helped him as Secretary of Transportation.

INTERPRETING WHAT YOU HAVE READ

1. Why might a person use racial fears to try to defeat someone else?

2. What effect do you think Peña's family had on his career choice?

3. Why do you think the dean of the University of Texas law school let Peña in, even though his test scores were low?

4. What do you think Peña's strategy was for battling the recall effort against him?

5. What do you think is Peña's formula for success?

ANALYZING QUOTATIONS

Read the following quotation from the biography and answer the questions below.

> *"There were no minorities on campus," Peña recalls. For the first time, "I ran into clear discrimination. There were people who wouldn't talk to me."*

1. Why do you think there were people who wouldn't talk to Peña on the campus?

2. How was Peña's response to this discrimination similar to the way he has dealt with other challenges in his life?

3. Why do you think people discriminate against others?

THINKING CRITICALLY

1. What do you think the slogan "Imagine a Great City" meant?

2. Do you think the voters who signed up for the "Peña" party are still voting? Why or why not?

3. If you had been Peña's political advisor, how would you have advised him to respond to his opponent's racist tactics?

4. Why do you think President Clinton chose Peña to be Transportation Secretary?

5. Politicians often write slogans that use a few words to tell what they believe. What might your slogan be?

ILEANA ROS-LEHTINEN

Ileana Ros-Lehtinen was the first woman and the first Latino to be elected to the U.S. House of Representatives. Born in Cuba, she feels that although Latinas are represented in all of the professions, they can still achieve more political power. In Congress, she devotes her attention to issues affecting human rights.

"**W**ell, all RIGHT!" Ileana Ros-Lehtinen (ee-leh-AH-nah rohs LEH-teh-nen) is likely to cheer when things are going her way. The Florida Congresswoman, who is the first Cuban and first Latina in Congress, is a whirl of action at the Capitol. "She has hit the ground running, and things are so much more lively around here since she arrived," says Representative Bill Paxon, a fellow Republican from New York. Ros-Lehtinen is a spark in the often staid[1] House of Representatives. She likes it that way. She's there to make her voice heard.

Some of Ros-Lehtinen's importance to the House comes from the qualities she adds to this largely white and male group. She sees things through the eyes of a female Cuban refugee concerned for her native country. As the only person in Congress with that viewpoint, Ros-Lehtinen feels a deep responsibility. For example, a bill that would have allowed U.S. farmers to sell rice to Cuba—and helped Fidel Castro's government—drew Ros-Lehtinen's fire. "As important as farmers in other states may be," she told the House, "I am wondering if the civil liberties[2] of the Cuban people are of any concern."

Her Cuban heritage has been a central part of Ros-Lehtinen's life since her birth in Cuba in 1952. She was born in Cuba's capital city, Havana, to Enrique Emilio Ros, an accountant, and Amanda Adato Ros. The family lived a comfortable life. Her father was a certified public accountant. Then, like many middle- and upper-class Cuban citizens, the Ros family left the island in 1960 after Fidel Castro's revolution succeeded and Cuba became a Communist society. The Ros family, including 7-year-

---

1. **staid** (STAYD) *adj.* serious; proper
2. **civil liberties** (SIH-vuhl LIH-buhr-teez) freedom from unnecessary government restrictions

old Ileana and her brother, went to Miami to join thousands of other Cubans. (See **Did You Know?** on page 186 for more information about the Cuban community in Miami.)

In Miami, Enrique Emilio Ros became involved with other refugees in planning the overthrow of Castro. When anti-Castro forces failed in their attempt in 1961, Ros realized that Cuba would probably not regain democratic rule in the near future. He vowed to raise his family as loyal U.S. citizens, making sure they never forgot their Cuban roots, language, and culture. According to Ros-Lehtinen's mother, Amanda, "He said you cannot educate two kids without a flag and a country. This is going to be their country and they have to love it."

Ros-Lehtinen graduated from high school, then earned an associate of arts degree at Miami-Dade Community College. Then she graduated from Florida International University in Miami with a degree in English. Ros-Lehtinen worked as a teacher and began a private school, Eastern Academy, in Miami. She was principal there for eight years. At the same time, she earned a master's degree with honors in education at Florida International University. She is still working on her doctorate in education at the University of Miami.

While doing all this, Ros-Lehtinen decided to run for Florida's state legislature. It was a decision largely influenced by her father, who had spent so much of his life concerned with the politics of his native country. Relying heavily on her father's political advice, Ros-Lehtinen was elected as a state representative in 1982. In 1986, she was elected state senator. During that time she met and married her husband, Dexter Lehtinen, who was also a Florida state legislator.

At first, she was concerned with global issues, but as her political experience grew, she became known as someone who was concerned with the little things that people want from their representatives in government. One political reporter in Miami called her "a pothole kind of legislator"—someone who would help citizens with everyday problems. That may be less glamorous than thinking about the world's problems, but for many citizens, it is more important.

In 1989, longtime U.S. Representative Claude Pepper died. Ros-Lehtinen decided that the House of Representatives needed a Cuban American voice. She resigned her state senate seat to run for the position of U.S. Representative from the 18th Congressional District of Florida. The fight for the vacant seat became one of the most vicious[3] in Florida history. The 18th district includes much of Miami and is 50 percent Latino. Gerald Richman, a white male attorney, won the Democratic primary election. Ros-Lehtinen and Richman would face one another for Pepper's seat in the House of Representatives.

The fight was bitter and fought largely along ethnic lines. It was also an important chance for the Republicans to gain a seat that had been in Democratic hands for 26 years. The race became a major issue when Republican party chair Lee Atwater said that, because the district was 50 percent Latino, electing a Cuban American was critical. The Democratic candidate, Gerald Richman, responded that the seat wasn't a Latino seat. "This is an American seat," he said.

Latinos reacted angrily, saying that they were as American as Richman was. The contest split along even stronger cultural lines. Spanish-language stations told their listeners that voting for Richman would be like voting for Castro. President Bush even got involved, traveling to Miami to give a speech for Ros-Lehtinen.

When the results of the intense election were finally in, Ros-Lehtinen had won with 53 percent of the vote. Ninety percent of Latinos had voted for her. Almost all African Americans and 96 percent of whites voted for Richman. Ros-Lehtinen had a huge job of soothing hurt feelings ahead. "It's been a terribly divisive[4] campaign," she said shortly after her victory. "But now it is the time for healing. I know that there are a lot of people out there who feel alienated."[5] Ros-Lehtinen has made progress

---

3. **vicious** (VIH-shuhs) *adj.* cruel; mean
4. **divisive** (duh-VEYE-sihv) *adj.* creating a lack of unity; causing to split apart
5. **alienated** (AY-lee-uh-nay-tuhd) *v.* to feel like one doesn't belong to a group

in healing these divisions. When she was up for reelection in 1990, she won with 60 percent of the vote. In 1992, 67 percent of the vote was cast for her.

Despite her pledge to deal with the concerns of all the people in her district, Ros-Lehtinen cannot forget that she is the only voice in the House for Cuban Americans. And she cannot forget her wish that Castro's rule would end in the tiny island country.

When a vote came up on a bill that would grant Nicaragua help in running fair elections, Ros-Lehtinen took an important step when she made her first speech to her fellow legislators. "I know what it is like to have the Communist thugs take away your home, your business, rip apart your family. But the main item that is missing in Nicaragua today is the one thing your vote can provide: Free, open, and democratic elections for all," she told them. "I only wish I would have a similar opportunity for my native Cuba." The other legislators applauded. It was unusual notice for a congresswoman's first effort.

She is unique as the only Republican on the Hispanic caucus[6] as well. "She will add a very important dimension to the caucus," says Rep. Bill Richardson, a New Mexico Democrat who is also a member of the Hispanic caucus, "because we've never had Cuban American input, which certainly exists and is a force in this country." Although Richardson is a Democrat, he had these words of praise for Ros-Lehtinen. "She shows enormous potential as a congresswoman. She seems also to have a good political feel for the House. She's engaging. She's articulate[7] and aggressive. About the only question mark might be whether she's too partisan.[8] And I don't know the answer yet."

Since she has arrived at the House of Representatives, Ros-Lehtinen has concentrated on the Foreign Affairs Committee,

---

6. **caucus** (KAW-kuhs) *n.* people who meet because they have common interests
7. **articulate** (ahr-TIH-kyuh-luht) *adj.* able to speak clearly and effectively
8. **partisan** (PAHR-tuh-zuhn) *adj.* strongly supporting one side, party, or person, sometimes unreasonably

with particular attention to issues affecting human rights and the western hemisphere.

Ros-Lehtinen stays close to her Miami roots. She tries to go home every week to see her husband and two young daughters, Amanda Michelle and Patricia Marie ("A.M. and P.M.," she calls them). She talks to them every day. She also talks to her husband, who is now an attorney in private practice in Miami, and to her father. She still considers her father her most important political guide. The members of her family, she says, are her best friends.

Ros-Lehtinen's busy life keeps her away from her family for long stretches, but the difficult separations are worth it, she says. In 1992, when accepting a special award from *Hispanic* magazine for her accomplishments, she said that the Latina "is an accomplished writer, or a computer programmer, or an attorney, or a doctor, as well as a loving wife and mother." Latinas, she writes, "must re-energize and refocus our efforts to realize the vast potential[9] that lies within our grasp."

> *Did You Know?* Since Miami is only 150 miles from Cuba, it was a natural choice for a new home for those who emigrated after Fidel Castro took power. During the early 1960s, almost 1,600 refugees a week came to the city. Today, a part of Miami is known as "Little Havana." The city is now bilingual, with a strong Cuban presence. More than 600,000 Cuban Americans—more than half of all of those in the United States—live in Dade County, where Miami is located.

---

9. **potential** (puh-TEHN-shuhl) *n.* a possibility; something that can develop

AFTER YOU READ

EXPLORING YOUR RESPONSES

1. If you were a member of the House of Representatives, what issues would you most like to work on? Why?

2. What do you think you would like most about being a legislator? What would you like least?

3. As a legislator, Ros-Lehtinen has had to speak often in public. What techniques can a speaker use to interest an audience?

4. Ros-Lehtinen has to be away from her children much of the time. How can a parent in this situation stay close to his or her children?

5. Imagine that you are giving a speech after winning your first election, and you want to thank the people who have helped you the most in your life. Whom would you thank? Why?

UNDERSTANDING WORDS IN CONTEXT

Read the following sentences from the biography. Think about what each underlined word means. In your notebook, write what the word means as it is used in the sentence.

1. Ros-Lehtinen is a spark in the often staid House of Representatives.

2. "It's been a terribly divisive campaign," she said shortly after her victory. "But now it is the time for healing."

3. "I know that there are a lot of people out there who feel alienated." Ros-Lehtinen has made progress in healing these divisions.

4. "She seems also to have a good political feel for the House. She's engaging. She's articulate and aggressive."

5. Latinas, she writes, "must re-energize and refocus our efforts to realize the vast potential that lies within our grasp."

RECALLING DETAILS

1. What new qualities does Ileana Ros-Lehtinen add to the U.S. House of Representatives?

2. Why did Ros-Lehtinen's family leave Cuba?

3. When did Enrique Emilio Ros decide that Cuba would not regain democracy in the near future?

4. Why was Ros-Lehtinen known as a "pothole kind of legislator"?

5. What is the most difficult part of being a member of Congress for Ros-Lehtinen?

UNDERSTANDING INFERENCES

In your notebook, write two or three sentences from the biography that support each of the following inferences.

1. Ileana Ros-Lehtinen's father does not believe in stereotyped sex roles.

2. Politics was an important part of life in the Ros household.

3. Members of both political parties are impressed by Ros-Lehtinen's performance in the House.

4. Her family continues to be important to Ros-Lehtinen.

5. Ros-Lehtinen has been successful in helping to heal the bad feelings from the 1989 campaign.

INTERPRETING WHAT YOU HAVE READ

1. Why do you think Ros-Lehtinen decided to enter politics?

2. Why do you think Ros-Lehtinen went from concentrating on global issues to "potholes" when she was in the Florida legislature?

3. How has Ros-Lehtinen's father influenced her career and her life?

4. Why do you think Latinos became so angry at hearing that the District 18 seat was "an American seat"?

5. Why do you think Ros-Lehtinen's fellow legislators applauded when she gave her first speech?

ANALYZING QUOTATIONS

Read the following quotation from the story and answer the questions below.

> Latinas, she writes, "must re-energize and refocus our efforts to realize the vast potential that lies within our grasp."

1. What "vast potential" do you think Ros-Lehtinen is talking about?

2. Why do you think Ros-Lehtinen thinks Latinas must "re-energize and refocus" their efforts?

3. How do you think someone could refocus his or her efforts to achieve a result?

THINKING CRITICALLY

1. What are some ways that Ros-Lehtinen could help heal the divisions in her community?

2. Do you think Ros-Lehtinen's status as the only Cuban American in Congress is a disadvantage or advantage? Explain your answer.

3. Why would Rep. Bill Richardson worry about Ros-Lehtinen being partisan?

4. Do you think Ros-Lehtinen will be a "pothole kind of legislator" in the House of Representatives, as she was in the Florida legislature? Explain.

5. Imagine that you are a representative. A poll has just been done in which you discover that almost everyone in your district disagrees with a stand you take. Explain why you will or will not change your position.

LINDA ALVARADO

Linda Alvarado, who owns Alvarado Construction, discusses a blueprint with a member of her staff. Alvarado, who is Mexican American, is one of the few Latinos to own a large construction company. She is also the first Latino to own a major league baseball team, the Colorado Rockies.

The construction project was big—a half million dollars—but Linda Alvarado (ahl-vah-RAH-doh) knew that her company was the best one for the job. She had even done a similar project. When Alvarado Construction didn't get the job, Linda Alvarado went back to the man in charge of making the decision and asked why.

He told her that she hadn't been in business very long. He said that her company wasn't big enough. Then, says Alvarado, "He leaned over and asked me, 'Does your mother know you're out doing this?' "

Now when Linda Alvarado tells this story, she thinks that it's funny. "You have to be able to have a good sense of humor and laugh it off," she says. It's also easier for her to laugh today. Her company has built everything from convention centers to office buildings to airport hangars. She runs a multi-million-dollar business that is one of the fastest-growing Latino enterprises in the country. It is an industry with few Latino owners, and even fewer women, in charge.

Alvarado didn't intend to spend her working life in a hard hat. She was born Linda Martinez in 1951 in Albuquerque, New Mexico, to a middle-class family. Her mother's Spanish ancestors had been in northern New Mexico since the days of Coronado. (See **Did You Know?** on page 195 for more information about the impact of Spanish explorers on the Americas.) Alvarado's mother was a homemaker. Her father came from a family of California farmers who moved to the United States from Mexico during the last century. He worked for the Atomic Energy Commission. When she was growing up, life was strict. Dinner was served every day at five, and after dinner everyone did homework. On Sundays the family went to church.

Even in what might seem a traditional environment, Alvarado says that she was expected to accomplish as much as her five brothers did. "Even though I was the only girl, the expectation for me was no different," she recalls. Her brothers did well in school sports. Alvarado did the same. She ran track and lettered in girls' basketball, volleyball, and softball.

Despite what might seem to be a carefree childhood, Alvarado remembers the sting of discrimination. In junior high school, her boyfriend's parents refused to let him see her after they learned her last name. On a high school choir tour of the Midwest and South, she remembers the signs that read "No Mexicans or Blacks Allowed." Alvarado credits her parents with giving their children the strength to stand up to bigotry. "Self-confidence was the greatest gift they gave us," she says.

Even though neither of Alvarado's parents went to college, they believed that college was important for their children. Linda thrilled them when she won a scholarship to Pomona College in California. She had never considered a career in construction, but, she landed her first job with a commercial developer, a company that arranged deals for constructing buildings. To her surprise, she became fascinated with the job. She liked overseeing construction and following the details of a building as it rose from the ground. One great advantage she had in this job, she says now, is that her boss "was lazy." He gave her more and more responsibility, and Alvarado got broader experience.

Before long, Alvarado was back in school to learn more about construction. In 1974, she formed her own company with an engineer from the firm where she had been working. Soon, she bought out the engineer. Her faith in herself was strong—it had to be. Before she established her company, Alvarado notes, "I never met or even heard of another woman contractor."

One source of support Alvarado found was her husband Robert Alvarado. On their first date, he took her to a Los Angeles Dodgers' game. He decided to marry her then, she says, because she was the first woman he had dated who dared to put onions on her hot dog. "Robert is not just my husband, but also my best friend," she says. "In those critical early years in business, he had great confidence in my ability and what I hoped to accomplish." Alvarado and her husband have two daughters and a son.

Finding the money to start up Alvarado Construction was almost impossible. She asked six banks for loans and was turned down each time. Finally, her parents loaned her $2,500, and she sold her car and mortgaged her house for more money. "I may have to go under or around or over," she explains, "but there's always a way of doing it."

As it turned out, gathering the money to start was the easy part. Four times she bid on jobs and was turned down. "They looked at me as a young woman and I was not taken seriously," she says. "This is also a field that Hispanics, unfortunately, have worked in primarily as laborers, so the lack of confidence was twofold."

When potential[1] clients looked at Alvarado and saw someone who couldn't do the job, she turned that sense of her difference into a positive. No one forgot the beautiful, determined young woman in the hard hat. Finally, her persistence[2] paid off.

When Alvarado couldn't get a job for her company, she sat down to think. People who weren't giving her work said that she didn't have the right experience. She decided to convince another construction company that they should bid for a job together. It was Alvarado Construction's showcase project. She did the work well and had one completed job to point to. Using that as evidence of her ability, Alvarado began to get work, did each job well, and her reputation grew.

Even today, with multi-million-dollar construction projects behind her, Alvarado says she sometimes meets people who doubt that she can do the job. "I hear, 'You're not tall enough. Women don't belong on a construction site.' I still hear these comments. I am concerned about other people's opinions, but I won't allow myself to be influenced by their ideas. I think this stops most people from accomplishing their goal."

More recently, Alvarado has gained attention for becoming another "first." She is the first Latino owner of a major league

---

1. **potential** (puh–TEHN–shuhl) *adj.* possible
2. **persistence** (puhr–SIHS–tuhnts) *n.* determination; continuing to work at something

baseball team. Her son, Alvarado says, was delighted by her decision. "We almost had to scrape him off the ceiling," she recalls. "He is a major Cubs fan." Alvarado's involvement was a big factor in major league baseball's awarding the Colorado Rockies franchise[3] to Denver. "She gives us something the other cities don't have, frankly," notes Paul Jacobs, who was also involved in getting major league baseball to choose Denver as an expansion site. "It's no secret that the major leagues have been emphasizing[4] minority participation and the participation of women in ownership."

For Alvarado, one of the most important parts of her entry into baseball is that "I am entering it with money that I earned. That's important." Also important for baseball, she believes, is her ability to bring her Latino background into the management of baseball. "Baseball has been a sport in which Hispanic players have achieved tremendous success," she says. "I think having a Hispanic team owner brings the sport full circle."

Sometimes financial success means that people distance themselves from their community. Not Alvarado. Along with her long list of multi-million-dollar projects and her investment in baseball, Alvarado has a shelf full of awards for leadership. In 1993, she was given the national Sara Lee Frontrunner Award. She was also named National Businesswoman of the Year by the U.S. Hispanic Chambers of Commerce. In addition, she has won awards for the hours she has spent inspiring young women who are interested in pursuing unconventional[5] careers.

"Once many of our ancestors were the country's business and government leaders," she says. "And once again, we are emerging as leaders in this country."

---

3. **franchise** (FRAN-cheyez) *n.* a right granted to sell something in a particular area
4. **emphasizing** (EHM-fuh-seyez-ihng) *v.* stressing; putting importance on
5. **unconventional** (uhn-kuhn-VEHN-shuhn-uhl) *adj.* out of the ordinary; not usual

Did You Know? *Some Latinos trace their roots to the Spanish explorers of the 1500s who came to North America. These explorers had three major influences on the Americas: language, religion, and culture. Spanish and English are the two dominant languages of the continent. The Spanish explorers did more than take a quick look around and head back to report to Spain. In the 1540s, Francisco Vásquez de Coronado explored the Colorado River, the Grand Canyon, and the Great Plains of what is now the United States. On the heels of Coronado were the Spanish settlers. They came to find their fortunes, to convert the Native Americans already there to Catholicism, and to administer the land for Spain. They built cities, such as Santa Fe, and the missions of California, such as San Diego. Their descendants are part of the Latino culture of this country.*

AFTER YOU READ

EXPLORING YOUR RESPONSES

1. Imagine that you own a business and someone asks if your mother knows you are doing this. How might you respond?

2. Alvarado says that the greatest gift her parents gave her was self-confidence. What other gifts can parents offer children?

3. Alvarado's parents expected as much from their daughter as from their sons. Do you think that parents should have the same or different expectations for their children?

4. Alvarado had trouble getting jobs for her new company, but she found a way to solve her problem. Describe a way that you or someone you know has solved a difficult problem.

5. Alvarado helps people who are considering unconventional careers. What unconventional career appeals to you? Why?

UNDERSTANDING WORDS IN CONTEXT

Read the following sentences from the biography. Think about what each underlined word means. In your notebook, write what the word means as it is used in the sentence.

1. When potential clients looked at Alvarado and saw someone who couldn't do the job, she turned that sense of her difference into a positive.

2. No one forgot the beautiful, determined young woman in the hard hat. Finally, her persistence paid off.

3. Alvarado's involvement was a big factor in major league baseball's awarding the Colorado Rockies franchise to Denver.

4. "It's no secret that the major leagues have been emphasizing minority participation and the participation of women. . . ."

5. She has also won awards for the hours she has spent inspiring young women who are interested in pursuing <u>unconventional</u> careers.

RECALLING DETAILS

1. What helped Alvarado face the bigotry she often experienced as a child?

2. How did Alvarado learn about the construction business?

3. List two reasons Alvarado had trouble being taken seriously as a contractor.

4. How did Alvarado get the first jobs for her new company?

5. Why does Alvarado think that her participation in major league baseball is important?

UNDERSTANDING INFERENCES

In your notebook, write two or three sentences from the biography that support each of the following inferences.

1. Linda Alvarado has spent her life breaking stereotypes.

2. Alvarado has been able to turn what could be considered problems into opportunities.

3. One of Linda Alvarado's greatest strengths is her persistence.

4. Alvarado's Latino heritage is important to her.

5. Alvarado feels that it is important to serve as a role model for young people.

INTERPRETING WHAT YOU HAVE READ

1. How did the values Alvarado's parents gave her help her later in her career?

2. How was Alvarado able to overcome the barriers against women and Latinos in construction projects?

3. In what ways do you think that Alvarado is different from other construction company owners? In what ways is she the same?

4. What advice do you think Alvarado would give a young person just starting out in his or her career?

5. Why do you think that Alvarado chose an unconventional profession like construction?

ANALYZING QUOTATIONS

Read the following quotation from the biography and answer the questions below.

"I am concerned about other people's opinions, but I won't allow myself to be influenced by their ideas. I think this stops most people from accomplishing their goal."

1. How could being concerned with other people's opinions stop someone from accomplishing a goal?

2. Name two times when Alvarado did not allow herself to be influenced by what other people thought.

3. Think of someone whose work you admire. How did that person achieve his or her goal?

THINKING CRITICALLY

1. How do you think Alvarado would respond today if she were asked, "Does your mother know what you're doing"?

2. Do you think that some jobs are better for men and others are better for women? Explain your answer.

3. Do you think that Alvarado has made a greater contribution as the owner of a construction business or as an owner of a major league baseball team? Explain.

4. Imagine that you were going to hire a contractor to build a house for you. What qualities would you look for?

5. Do you think that you would be willing to go through what Alvarado did to become successful? Why or why not?

ROBERTO GOIZUETA

Roberto Goizueta, chairman of Coca Cola, samples his product in Atlanta on the occasion of his tenth anniversary with the company. The Cuban-born businessman used lessons he learned from his grandfather to help him succeed in the business world. Goizueta is now thought to be the third-richest Latino in the United States.

Introduce a new Coca-Cola product? Impossible. Coke is unique, company managers said angrily. A competing Coke product would fail. Cuban-born Roberto Goizueta (goi-SWEH-tah),Coca-Cola's new chairman, heard all the arguments. Then he quietly gave the go-ahead.

In July of 1982, the first new product to carry the Coca-Cola name was introduced. The employees at the company held their breath. They didn't need to worry. Diet Coke became an instant best-seller. Within a year, it was the fourth most popular soft drink in the United States. Today, it is the third most popular soft drink in the world. Experts consider diet Coke to be the most successful new product of the 1980s. Roberto Goizueta, the reserved, quiet man from Cuba, had begun to bring a fading U.S. institution, Coca-Cola, back to life. Pepsi-Cola, which had been threatening to take the crown of the best-loved soft drink, was once again banished[1] to second place.

Goizueta was born in Cuba in 1931 to a family that became wealthy growing, harvesting, and selling sugar cane. His family lived in his grandfather's mansion. It was a culture in which elders were respected, a strict and traditional upbringing. Goizueta spent hours with his grandfather, listening to his stories and his sayings. Later, as an executive, he would use these Cuban proverbs[2] to make a point. One of his favorites, a natural for a business executive who often must make critical decisions, is: "The quality of one's compromises is much more important than the correctness of one's position."

When Goizueta was a senior in high school, he attended Cheshire Academy in Connecticut. It was a prep school for the wealthy. The students were expected to attend the best colleges

---

1. **banished** (BA-nihsht) *v.* driven out
2. **proverbs** (PRAHV-uhrbz) *n. pl.* brief sayings containing wisdom

in the country and to study hard to get there. Goizueta's problem was that he spoke no English. The 18-year-old spent "many sleepless nights studying the dictionary," he says. "My professor said my sentence structure was textbook-perfect. It should have been. It came right out of the textbook." Besides studying the dictionary, Goizueta spent many hours watching movies and memorizing dialogue and U.S. attitudes.

By the end of the year, Goizueta did more than speak English. He was the valedictorian[3] of his class. That fall he went to Yale University to study chemical engineering. After graduation in 1954, he answered an ad for a chemical engineer's position in Havana, Cuba. He got the job as a chemist in charge of making sure that the quality of Coke stayed high. Through the next few years, Goizueta climbed the corporate ladder of the organization. He worked in Nassau as head of Coke's Caribbean operation, then became second in charge of the entire Latin American division.

Today, Cuba is one of the few countries in the world in which you can't buy a Coke. Goizueta has said that if Fidel Castro had not taken power, his father probably would have bought the Havana Coca-Cola bottling plant for his son to run. (See *Did You Know?* on page 204 for more information about Fidel Castro.) Instead of inheriting family wealth and position, Goizueta made his own way—and made it big. Rather than running a small island operation, today he is running Coca-Cola worldwide.

When Robert Woodruff, who had been Coke's leader since 1923, asked Roberto Goizueta to become the next CEO (Chief Executive Officer)[4] of Coca-Cola, Goizueta responded with the deference[5] he had had for his Cuban grandfather. "Well, Mr. Woodruff," he said, "I'd be flattered." Goizueta and Woodruff had an almost father-and-son relationship. Goizueta treated

---

3. **valedictorian** (va-luh-dihk-TOHR-ee-uhn) *n.* the student, usually with the highest grades, who gives the address at a graduation ceremony
4. **Chief Executive Officer** the leader of an organization or business
5. **deference** (DEH-fuhr-ruhns) *n.* respect due an older or wiser person

Woodruff as he had treated his grandfather, and the older man appreciated that. But when Woodruff handed Goizueta the prize of leadership, some in the company were surprised. The new CEO was Cuban, after all, and Coke is the most American of companies.

Robert Woodruff was doing more than just choosing a younger man who treated him with respect. He understood that the Coke of the future would not simply be a U.S. company. Goizueta understands that, too. At one time, he says, Coke was a U.S. company that did business in other countries. "Now we are a large international company with a sizable American business," he notes. The United States may be Coca-Cola's home, but Coke is as international as any product in the world. Many people think that Goizueta, with his ability to speak Spanish as well as English, and his background in Latin America, is the model international businessman and the perfect person to lead Coke into its increasingly international future.

Goizueta did more than introduce diet Coke to the world. When he took over, Goizueta says, "the company had no sense of direction whatsoever. None." The company was drifting into other businesses without much reason. It was disorganized. There was little sense of which parts of the business made money and which lost money. Goizueta "stayed home to clean out the stables," he says. Under his direction, Coke sold off unprofitable operations and reorganized those that remained so he could see if they were making or losing money. Under his command, Coke boosted sales by changing its bland slogan "Have a Coke and a smile" to the punchy "Coke is it!" Goizueta bought Columbia Pictures for Coke in 1982, a move that many thought was a mistake. Goizueta proved the wisdom of his actions, though, when he sold Columbia in 1989 for $1.55 billion, a profit of $858 million.

Next came what many business watchers consider the biggest business mistake of the century. For years, Coke sales had been flat, with Pepsi nipping at the leader's heels. After spending millions on research to come up with a new formula, Goizueta and Coke announced in 1985 that they were changing the formula of the most famous soft drink in the world.

The uproar from U.S. Coke drinkers took everyone by surprise. "Changing Coke is just like breaking the American dream, like not selling hot dogs at a ball game," wrote one of the furious thousands of Coke fans. Enraged[6] Coke drinkers dumped New Coke in the river. One customer even sued to get the old Coke back.

To his credit, Goizueta took full responsibility for the disaster in a press conference. The old Coke would return, Goizueta announced. Soon it was back on the shelves, and thousands of thank-you letters poured in. "I feel like a lost friend is returning home," read one. Another fan of old Coke hired an airplane to circle above the company's office with a banner that read "THANK YOU ROBERTO."

The response was so immediate that some even accused Coke of planning the whole thing. That wasn't true, but by the time the Coke "war" was over, the results must have made Goizueta very happy. In 1986, the hundredth anniversary of the most famous soft drink in the world, Coke had widened its lead over rival[7] Pepsi. Coke had 39 percent of the market for soft drinks in the United States, while Pepsi had 28 percent.

Goizueta's moves at Coca-Cola have worked. When he took over the company in 1980, its value was $4 billion. In 1992, the company was worth $56 billion. Today, it is the sixth most valuable company in the United States.

One reason for the company's huge jump in value has been Goizueta's interest in making Coca-Cola a truly international company. Right now, every man, woman, and child in the United States drinks an average of 296 Coke products a year. In China, the company hopes to sell everyone 217 Cokes a year. If the company can do that, Goizueta foresees that in China "We will have another company the size of the Coca-Cola Company

---

6. **enraged** (ihn-RAYJD) *adj.* angered
7. **rival** (REYE-vuhl) *adj.* competitor

today"—in effect, a Coca-Cola double the size of the current company.

Goizueta is a private man. His interests outside the company are his family, reading everything he can find, swimming, and down-home country music. He is also involved with many charities. He is the founding director of the Points of Light Initiative, which recognizes and encourages charitable work throughout the United States.

The Coca-Cola Company is still the passion of Roberto Goizueta's life. His worth is estimated at $245 million, mostly in Coke stock, making him the third-richest Latino in this country, but he shows no interest in slowing down. He is also one of the most-respected business leaders in the world. "Goizueta has been one of the best-performing CEOs in U.S. business," wrote *Fortune* magazine in 1992. Like his product, Roberto Goizueta is a true American success story.

> **Did You Know?** *Fidel Castro, who was born in Cuba in 1929, was the leader of the campaign in Cuba to overthrow the dictator Fulgencio Batista (fool-HEN-see-oh bah-TEES-tah). In 1959, Castro succeeded in his revolution against Batista and set up a Communist government that favored the working class and poor Cubans. He seized businesses and farms that were privately owned and declared them the property of all the people. As a result, many middle- and upper-class Cubans emigrated in 1959 and 1960, immediately after Castro took power.*

EXPLORING YOUR RESPONSES

1. Goizueta decided to introduce diet Coke even though many thought he was wrong. What might you have done in his place?

2. Goizueta spent many hours as a young person with his grandfather. Describe an older person who has had a big impact on your life.

3. To learn English, Goizueta studied the dictionary and watched movies. How might you learn another language?

4. If you had been responsible for introducing New Coke, what might you have done after it became unpopular?

5. What U.S. product would you like to sell internationally? Why?

UNDERSTANDING WORDS IN CONTEXT

Read the following sentences from the biography. Think about what each underlined word means. In your notebook, write what the word means as it is used in the sentence.

1. Pepsi-Cola, which had been threatening to take the crown of the best-loved soft drink, was once again banished to second place.

2. Goizueta spent hours with his grandfather, listening to his stories and his sayings. Later, as an executive, he would use these Cuban proverbs to make a point.

3. When Robert Woodruff, who had been Coke's leader since 1923, asked Roberto Goizueta to become the next CEO (Chief Executive Officer) of Coca-Cola, Goizueta responded with the deference he had had for his Cuban grandfather.

4. Enraged Coke drinkers dumped New Coke in the river.

5. In 1986, the hundredth anniversary of the most famous soft drink in the world, Coke had widened its lead over rival Pepsi.

RECALLING DETAILS

1. How did Roberto Goizueta learn English?

2. Where might Goizueta be today if Castro had not overthrown the government of Cuba?

3. Why did Robert Woodruff choose Goizueta to run Coca-Cola?

4. List two of Goizueta's major successes at Coke.

5. How did Goizueta recover from the New Coke disaster?

UNDERSTANDING INFERENCES

In your notebook, write two or three sentences from the biography that support each of the following inferences.

1. Roberto Goizueta likes to take chances.

2. Goizueta wanted to make his own way in the world, without relying on his family's money.

3. Goizueta's Cuban background has had a strong influence on his career.

4. The fear that Pepsi might outsell Coke may have led Goizueta to make a major business mistake.

5. The business world agrees with the changes that Goizueta has made in the Coca-Cola company.

INTERPRETING WHAT YOU HAVE READ

1. What qualities do you think have made Roberto Goizueta successful?

2. What qualities do you think are most important for a good international business leader?

3. What lessons do you think the New Coke disaster taught Roberto Goizueta?

4. Compare the success of diet Coke and the failure of New Coke. What do you think made one product succeed while the other failed?

5. How might Goizueta have avoided the New Coke disaster?

ANALYZING QUOTATIONS

Read the following quotation from the biography and answer the questions below.

"The quality of one's compromises is much more important than the correctness of one's position."

1. Why would a businessperson find this advice useful?

2. What evidence do you see in Goizueta's career that he followed this proverb?

3. When do you think that it would make more sense to compromise than to hold onto a correct position?

THINKING CRITICALLY

1. Do you agree that Goizueta would have remained in Cuba running Coca-Cola if Castro had not taken over Cuba? Explain.

2. How might Goizueta's grandfather's stories and sayings have helped prepare his grandson for the business world?

3. Do you think that someone who is a good business leader in the United States would automatically be a good leader for a global company? Explain your answer.

4. Goizueta's Points of Light Initiative encourages charitable work. How do you think people can encourage others to help each other and the environment?

5. Roberto Goizueta does not like to talk publicly about his life. How can publicity affect a person's life?

OSCAR DE LA RENTA

Fashion designer Oscar de la Renta shows his 1993 spring/summer high fashion collection in Paris. Born in the Dominican Republic, de la Renta was the first U.S. designer to show his collection in Paris.

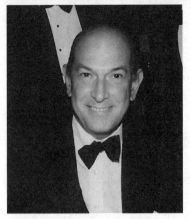

PARIS, 1991. Beautiful women floated down the runway, twirling in expensive silk gowns as the crowd watched. It may have looked like just another fashion show, but backstage, tension was high. This wasn't just another show. This was the first time an American had presented his clothes in France, the world center of fashion. If Oscar de la Renta's (day lah REN-tah) show wasn't a smash, it would be a huge blow to his prestige.[1]

The show ended and the crowd, American and French alike, exploded in applause, standing to honor de la Renta. The phones began ringing with orders for the collection. The designer's gamble had paid off.

Oscar de la Renta, the tall, impeccably[2] dressed native of the Dominican Republic, has blazed a trail across the U.S. fashion scene. He is said to understand what women want and what men want to look at. He has turned that feeling for beauty into an empire that today sells more than $500 million in dresses, accessories, and perfume every year. The secret, de la Renta says, is "to still have the passion to do it. I love what I do."

De la Renta was born in the Dominican Republic in 1932 and grew up there. He was the youngest child, with six older sisters and a very protective mother. "She was very loving and sometimes very strict," de la Renta says. "I was often frustrated because I wasn't allowed to play in the street like other boys." His father was in the insurance business and the elder de la Renta expected his son to follow him. "I had absolutely zero interest in it," de la Renta says. "All I wanted was to become a painter."

When he was 18, his mother was dying of multiple sclerosis. She knew that her husband would not allow their son to leave

---

1. **prestige** (preh-STEEZH) *n.* standing in the community
2. **impeccably** (ihm-PEH-kuh-blee) *adv.* perfectly; without error

the island after her death, so she made what de la Renta called "the ultimate[3] sacrifice." She convinced her husband to allow Oscar to leave the Dominican Republic to study art. "She realized that she would never see me again," de la Renta says.

De la Renta traveled to the United States to study art, and then to Spain. His father still wanted him to return, so de la Renta tried to convince him that he could make a living at his art. "I started doing fashion illustration for newspapers and magazines in Spain because I could draw very well. That led me into the fashion houses," he recalls.

Once he began working for the Spanish fashion industry, de la Renta became intrigued by the world of fine fabrics and glamorous gowns. Although he had never studied fashion, he watched closely "how clothes were made, how they were cut, how they were constructed. And so then I said, 'Well, perhaps I can be a fashion designer and paint sometime.' " Finally, after years of doing both, de la Renta gave up painting. "To do something very well, you have to do only one thing," he says.

De la Renta landed in the Spanish office of Cristobal Balenciaga (bah-len-see-AH-gah), a man de la Renta calls "probably the greatest designer of our time." From there, he moved to the Paris house of Lanvin, another fashion legend. De la Renta had even bigger plans, though. At a dinner party in New York City in 1963, he charmed designer Elizabeth Arden. She hired him to create clothes for her.

The next year, in Paris, Oscar de la Renta met and fell in love with Françoise de Langlade (lahn-GLAHD), the editor of Paris *Vogue*. Within months, they married and moved to New York City. Together, the beautiful, powerful editor and the tall, handsome de la Renta made a stir in New York. They hosted glittering dinner parties in their fashionable New York apartment that attracted European royalty and U.S. politicians.

By 1966, de la Renta had his own line[4] of clothes. The next

---

3. **ultimate** (UL-tuh-muht) *adj.* highest; most extreme
4. **line** *n.* collection of clothing designs

year, he won fashion's Coty award, the most important award a U.S. designer can capture. The designer from the Dominican Republic became known for his use of color and for his rich, luxurious[5] evening clothes. He developed a perfume, called Oscar de la Renta, that now accounts for about one third of his income. It seemed that de la Renta's life would continue with one triumph after another. But in 1983, his beloved wife died.

A lonely de la Renta plunged into his work. Before long he had a new, unexpected passion to occupy him. In 1982, he was asked to contribute to a program that would offer classes to street children in the Dominican Republic. "I said, of course I will help you. It was really a very, very small budget, very little money. We started with 8 children. Today we are taking care of about 350 children on a daily basis," de la Renta says. "It gives me tremendous pleasure, and it gives me a perspective[6] of what life is really all about."

Two years after his wife's death, de la Renta was still lonely. He was spending as much time as he could at the school. One day, workers there found an abandoned baby who had been tossed on a garbage heap. The baby weighed two pounds. "Talking to the doctor, I said, 'What do you think would be the best thing for him?' " de la Renta recalls. The doctor told de la Renta to find the baby Moises (MOI-sehs) a good home. He had been named by the nurses at the school. The baby had reminded them of the Biblical figure of Moses, who had also been abandoned.

"At that point, in my heart I knew I couldn't see him go, so I took him home with me, because he had a very bad cold. But in my mind I knew he was going to stay there." De la Renta put a crib in his own room, brought Moises home and adopted him. "I have 14 servants, but I fed him, washed him, and changed his nappies [diapers] myself. And I decided he must stay."

---

5. **luxurious** (luhg-ZHOOR-ee-uhs) *adj.* of the finest and richest kind; elegant
6. **perspective** (puhr-SPEHK-tihv) *n.* the ability to see the true importance of things

Today, Moises lives in de la Renta's Connecticut home and attends school nearby. "Moises and I found each other at a time in our lives when we most needed each other," de la Renta says. "I will create for him the opportunities he needs, but I am not an American parent. I don't want to push him. One of the doctors once said to me, 'There is only one thing that you can do for Moises, and that is to love him.' "

In 1989, de la Renta was married again, to heiress[7] Annette Reed. The designer's second wife is more private than Françoise was. "Oscar adores people," Annette says. "I don't, in the same way. He's open, generous, and loving. I'm private, dread going out, hate dressing up. I would rather weed. And I'm not stylish." Even so, the family lives a life that fits de la Renta's love of beauty and luxury. They spend time in their rambling Connecticut house, in their lavishly[8] decorated apartment in New York, and in their two houses in the Dominican Republic. One of the houses is on a working plantation on the island. The house there is open to tropical breezes scented by the 2,500 acres of orange and passion fruit trees that surround the house. Each room is painted a different color.

Although he is a U.S. citizen, de la Renta still plays an important role in his native country. (See **Did You Know?** on page 213 for more information about Dominican immigration and U.S. citizenship.) "There is no way you can escape it. It is such a small country that one voice makes a difference," he said.

"I left the Dominican Republic, really, when I was eighteen years old, and I have never really lived there since that time," said de la Renta, "but still, in my heart, I am very much a Dominican."

---

7. **heiress** (AR-uhs) *n.* a woman whose family is wealthy
8. **lavishly** (LA-vihsh-lee) *adv.* richly; expensively

Did You Know? Although Dominicans are often compared to Puerto Ricans and Cubans because all three peoples are from islands in the Caribbean, each group has a very different relationship to the United States. Puerto Ricans are born citizens of this country and Cubans are often granted citizenship because they are fleeing a Communist state. Dominicans can claim neither of these special conditions. People from the Dominican Republic who immigrate must be permanent residents for five years before they can apply for citizenship, and many are denied because of restrictions on the number of immigrants who can enter the United States.

AFTER YOU READ

EXPLORING YOUR RESPONSES

1. Do you think fashion is an important subject? Explain.

2. Oscar de la Renta says his mother was strict, loving, and protective. What three qualities do you think are most important for parents to have?

3. De la Renta's father wanted him to be an insurance agent and his mother wanted him to choose his own career. How do you think parents should help their children make a career choice?

4. Do you agree with de la Renta that "to do something very well, you have to do only one thing"? Explain.

5. De la Renta saw a need for a school for poor children in the Dominican Republic. What need do you see in your community? How might you fill it?

UNDERSTANDING WORDS IN CONTEXT

Read the following sentences from the biography. Think about what each <u>underlined</u> word means. In your notebook, write what the word means as it is used in the sentence.

1. If Oscar de la Renta's show wasn't a smash, it would be a huge blow to his <u>prestige</u>.

2. Oscar de la Renta, the tall, <u>impeccably</u> dressed native of the Dominican Republic, has blazed a trail across the U.S. fashion scene.

3. The designer from the Dominican Republic became known for his use of color and for his rich, <u>luxurious</u> evening clothes.

4. "Today we are taking care of about 350 children on a daily basis," de la Renta says. "It gives me tremendous pleasure, and it gives me a <u>perspective</u> of what life is really all about."

5. They spend time in their rambling Connecticut house, in their <u>lavishly</u> decorated apartment in New York, and in their two houses in the Dominican Republic.

RECALLING DETAILS

1. Why was de la Renta's Paris show in 1991 a big gamble?
2. Why does de la Renta think he is so successful?
3. How did de la Renta try to convince his father that he could make a career of art?
4. Why did de la Renta take Moises home?
5. How did de la Renta choose a career in fashion?

UNDERSTANDING INFERENCES

In your notebook, write two or three sentences that support each of the following inferences.

1. U.S. designers had not been successful in France until de la Renta presented his line of clothing.
2. Oscar de la Renta is self-confident.
3. De la Renta sometimes felt restricted by his parents.
4. De la Renta gradually realized how important the children's program in the Dominican Republic was to him.
5. Unlike his father, de la Renta will probably not expect his son to enter his profession.

INTERPRETING WHAT YOU HAVE READ

1. Why did de la Renta's mother make what he called "the ultimate sacrifice"?
2. De la Renta says the school he is involved with in the Dominican Republic "gives me a perspective of what life is really all about." What do you think that perspective is?
3. Why do you think de la Renta believes that he needed to give up painting to become a successful designer?

4. De la Renta says he is not an "American parent." How do you think he would describe an American parent?

5. Why do you think de la Renta says he is still a Dominican after not having lived there for so many years?

ANALYZING QUOTATIONS

Read the following quotation from the biography and answer the questions below.

> "There is no way you can escape it [playing an important role in the Dominican Republic]. It is such a small country that one voice makes a difference."

1. What do you think de la Renta means when he says he cannot escape playing an important role in his native country?

2. Do you think de la Renta's voice would make more of a difference than other voices in the Dominican Republic? Explain your answer.

3. Do you think your voice makes a difference in your community or your school? Why or why not?

THINKING CRITICALLY

1. De la Renta says his mother was protective. What do you think are the advantages and disadvantages of having a protective parent?

2. What were the key ingredients to de la Renta's success?

3. If he hadn't begun drawing fashion illustrations, what do you think de la Renta would have done? Why?

4. What do you think Moises brought to de la Renta's life?

5. Do you think de la Renta would have become involved in another charitable organization in the Dominican Republic if he had not been asked to contribute to the children's program? Explain your answer.

ANTONIA HERNÁNDEZ

Attorney Antonia Hernández is shown in her office at the Mexican American Legal Defense and Education Fund (MALDEF) in Los Angeles. Hernández fights to assure that Mexican Americans like herself, and all Latinos, achieve equal treatment under the law.

Her path was clear, Antonia Hernández (ahn-TOHN-ee-ah er-NAHN-des) thought. Like several of her aunts and cousins, she would become a teacher. She graduated from college in 1970 and then earned her teaching credentials from the Graduate School of Education at the University of California at Los Angeles (UCLA). She was counseling high school students in East Los Angeles at the same time. Then the students began to stage walkouts to protest the poor conditions and the lack of educational opportunities at their schools. Hernández agreed with them. Gradually, she found that she "realized that we couldn't help the kids as teachers unless we did something about the laws that were holding them back." These laws, she felt, kept the students from receiving a good education.

It is now almost 25 years later, and Hernández is one of the most important Latino leaders in the country. As it was then, her focus is clear. She practices law to help Latinos.

Hernández was born in 1948 in the Mexican state of Coahuila (koh-ah-OOEE-lah). When she was 8, her family moved to East Los Angeles. Hernández's father, Manuel, worked in light industry. Her mother, Nicolasa, worked in a nursery. Hernández had six younger brothers and sisters she helped care for. Nicolasa had unusual dreams for her children, particularly her daughters. "In my time, women didn't have the freedom that women have today," she says. "But I wanted my daughters to have that, to learn, to travel, to work, to do whatever they wanted to do."

"I grew up in a very happy environment,[1] but a very poor environment," Hernández says. It was also an environment in which pride was important. When graffiti appeared on their

---

1. **environment** (ihn-VEYE-ruhn-muhnt) *n.* the conditions that affect the way a plant, animal, or person develops

housing project, Nicolasa Hernández made her children scrub it off immediately. The rest of the neighborhood might be vandalized, but the Hernández family's building would be clean.

Because she came to the United States as an 8-year-old, Hernández already had a sense of her culture firmly in place. "When I came to the United States, I was very proud of who I was. I was a Mexican, I had an identity,[2] I had been taught a history, a culture of centuries of rich civilization," she says. "My father always taught us that we could accomplish anything based on hard work and pride of who we were and where we came from. Those were very Mexican values, but they were also very American values."

Education was another value that Hernández's parents stressed. When she and her family arrived in Los Angeles, she spoke no English and was thrown into an English-speaking classroom. (See *Did You Know?* on page 222 for more information about Spanish speakers in the United States.) She struggled, but she did learn English. "I made it," she says of her days as a non-English speaker in an English-speaking classroom. "But just because I made it cannot be used as an example that it works." Today, Hernández is a firm believer in bilingual[3] education as the best way for non-English speakers to keep their original language, keep their pride in their culture, and learn English.

She also admires her father for insisting that his family be exposed to as much education as possible. "Even though we were poor economically,[4] we were always exposed to learning," she says. Occasionally, her father would take the family to the Salvation Army store, where he would buy old copies of *National Geographic* magazine so that his children could read and learn from them.

Because the family was poor, everyone who could work helped out. Hernández remembers picking crops in the summer

---

2. **identity** (eye-DEHN-tuh-tee) *n.* the collection of qualities that makes a person different from others
3. **bilingual** (beye-LIHNG-wuhl) *adj.* using two languages
4. **economically** (eh-kuh-NAH-mih-kuh-lee) *adv.* having to do with money

during her school years. The Hernández children learned the importance of education. They all graduated from college. Several became teachers, as Antonia Hernández set out to do. "My parents instilled[5] in us the belief that serving the public interest was a very noble thing to do," she says.

Once she decided to go to law school, her teachers encouraged her to apply to a well-known school like Harvard or Stanford. Hernández decided not to do that. She wanted to stay close to her family so she went to law school at UCLA. "I was the oldest in our family, and my parents were sacrificing[6] everything they could to help me with school," she says. "They were looking forward to me graduating and working as a teacher so I could help them with the rest of the kids. So my feeling was that if I were to ask them to sacrifice three more years, moving away would be too drastic."

Even while she was in law school, Hernández was involved in public service. She worked with the college's admissions committee and Chicano student organizations. "To me, to be a really good lawyer, you have to be a well-rounded person," she says. While in law school, Hernández began spending time with Michael Stern, another lawyer who also wanted to use the law for social justice. They married in 1977.

True to her word, when Hernández graduated and became a lawyer, she immediately became involved in public interest law, or law that is intended to help change society. She found a job at the East Los Angeles Center for Law and Justice. Often, her work there involved issues such as police brutality[7] toward minorities. Then she became the head attorney for the Lincoln Heights Office of the Legal Aid Foundation, which provides services to those who are too poor to afford them.

In 1978, Hernández received an offer that showed that her work was becoming widely recognized. She was asked to be the

---

5. **instilled** (ihn-STIHLD) *v.* put in little by little
6. **sacrificing** (SAK-ruh-feyes-ihng) *v.* giving up
7. **brutality** (broo-TA-luh-tee) *n.* cruelty

first Latino to work for the important United States Judiciary Committee in Washington, D.C.

For Hernández, it was a difficult decision. Her husband told her to take the job. "We didn't have children," he remembers. "We had very little furniture and few responsibilities. I figured I'd get a job."

At first, Hernández said no. She couldn't bear the thought of leaving her home. "I was very happy doing poverty law and being near my family," she says. Then the committee called back and offered more money. "I didn't want to explain what the problem was, so I said yes."

Hernández found a different world in Washington. Despite her involvement in her community in California, "The most political thing I had ever done before that job was to vote," she says. In Washington, she helped write legislation and informed members of the Senate about civil rights[8] and immigration issues.

In 1980, the Democrats lost control of the Senate. Hernández lost her job, but the Mexican American Legal Defense and Education Fund (MALDEF) in Los Angeles offered her a job within days. She took it. It was a perfect fit. MALDEF has a long history of success working for the Latino community in this country.

MALDEF was formed in 1968 after a Latino lawyer was angered because he felt that a client could not get a fair trial with no Latinos on the jury. Today, MALDEF has an annual budget of $5 million and 22 attorneys. It is considered one of the most effective organizations pressing for Latino rights.

In 1985, Hernández became the president of MALDEF. "I run a business," she says. "This business is about change." Among the victories during her presidency is the decision by the U.S. Supreme Court that Latinos were not represented in voting districts in Los Angeles. That victory led to the election of the

---

8. **civil rights** the rights of personal liberty granted by the U.S. Constitution and acts of Congress

first Latino to serve on the Los Angeles County Board of Supervisors, which governs an area more populated than most states. Another lawsuit MALDEF won in Texas ensured that all children there, whether they are from a poor or a rich school district, have the same amount of money spent on their education.

Hernández feels that the 1990s is an important decade for Latinos. "We need to move," she says. "Otherwise, we'll develop into a community with a small middle class and a large underclass."

She still feels the strong pull of family. "I try to balance my life and it has worked," Hernández says. "But I have little time for myself or my good friends." She and her husband have three children, whom Hernández calls "my greatest accomplishment." She has tried to keep their children deeply aware of their Mexican–Jewish heritage and the richness it can bring to their lives. "I tell them that by knowing more than one language and staying in touch with their culture, they are going to be much more learned, much more valuable as human beings."

> **Did You Know?** Spanish is the most common language spoken in the United States, aside from English. Nine out of ten people in this country who come from a Spanish-speaking country say that they speak Spanish at home. Children who only spoke Spanish were once thrown into classrooms where no Spanish was spoken. Today, thanks to cases MALDEF brought in the 1970s and 1980s, federal courts have ruled that bilingual education is a constitutional right.

AFTER YOU READ

EXPLORING YOUR RESPONSES

1. Do you think school conditions can influence the way children learn? Explain.

2. When she was growing up, Hernández's father would buy used copies of *National Geographic* so his children could learn from them. What other ways can people learn without spending much money?

3. Hernández grew up believing that serving the public interest was a noble thing to do. What do you consider to be a noble occupation? Why?

4. Hernández decided to stay in California to go to law school instead of going to a better-known school in the East. What might you have done?

5. How can politics make a difference in people's lives?

UNDERSTANDING WORDS IN CONTEXT

Read the following sentences from the biography. Think about what each underlined word means. In your notebook, write what the word means as it is used in the sentence.

1. "I grew up in a very happy environment, but a very poor environment," Hernández says.

2. "I was a Mexican, I had an identity, I had been taught a history, a culture of centuries of rich civilization," she says.

3. Today, Hernández is a firm believer in bilingual education as the best way for non-English speakers to keep their original language, keep their pride in their culture, and learn English.

4. "My parents instilled in us the belief that serving the public interest was a very noble thing to do," she said.

5. "I was the oldest in our family, and my parents were sacrificing everything they could to help me with school," she says.

RECALLING DETAILS

1. Why did Hernández decide to change careers from teaching to law?

2. How did Hernández's parents help her become the person she is today?

3. What kind of law did Hernández decide to go into?

4. Why did Hernández almost turn down the job working for the U.S. Judiciary Committee?

5. Name two important victories MALDEF has had.

UNDERSTANDING INFERENCES

In your notebook, write two or three sentences from the biography that support each of the following inferences.

1. Hernández's parents' values influenced her choice of career.

2. Hernández's law work puts her principles into action.

3. Having a sense of cultural pride can be an advantage.

4. Hernández has put her family ahead of her career and her social life.

5. Hernández is passing on to her children the same values she learned from her parents.

INTERPRETING WHAT YOU HAVE READ

1. What characteristics most helped Hernández get where she is today?

2. Why do you think all of Hernández's sisters and brothers went to college?

3. Why do you think MALDEF offered Hernández a job so quickly?

4. Why do you think Hernández is considered one of the most important Latino leaders in the country?

5. How would you characterize the victories MALDEF has won for the Latino people?

ANALYZING QUOTATIONS

Read the following quotation from the biography and answer the questions below.

> *"I tell them that by knowing more than one language and staying in touch with their culture, they are going to be much more learned, much more valuable as human beings."*

1. How could staying in touch with their culture help Hernández's children be more valuable as human beings?

2. Why do you think Hernández has these goals for her children?

3. Name some ways that people can stay in touch with their culture.

THINKING CRITICALLY

1. Do you think a person could have more impact as a teacher or a lawyer? Explain your answer.

2. Do you believe bilingual education is a good or bad idea? Defend your answer.

3. Do you think Hernández's mother or father had more impact on the choices she made as an adult? Explain your answer.

4. What sacrifices do you think Hernández has to make to be successful at her job? Explain whether you think the results outweigh the sacrifices.

5. If a friend had a conflict between family and career, how would you suggest he or she resolve it?

CULTURAL CONNECTIONS

Thinking About What People Do

1. Several of the people in this unit changed their minds about the kind of work they wanted to do. Compare two of them and point out how their reasons for changing careers were similar and different.

2. Write an editorial for your school newspaper stating how people in business or in public service can help others. How can they use their business or office to make a difference? As you write your opinion, use one or two of the subjects of this unit as examples. You may also refer to people in your community who are in these fields.

3. Design a business card for one company you read about in this unit or for another company, real or imaginary. Write one or two short phrases to promote your company. Draw a picture or logo on the card, if you wish.

Thinking About Culture

1. Imagine that you were childhood friends with one of the subjects in this unit. Write what you observed about the subject's family life and tell how you think it influenced his or her life and work.

2. All of the people you read about in this unit feel strong ties to their native cultures. Discuss the ways that two subjects joined their first culture with U.S. culture.

3. Many of the subjects of these biographies are involved, through business or government, with countries around the world. Choose two people and give examples that show how the influence of their cultural heritage has made them "international citizens."

Building Research Skills

Work with a partner to complete the following activity.

Three of the biographies in this unit feature people who are in business. Choose one whose company interests you or select another business owner or company you would like to learn about. Write a list of questions about that business. You might begin with the following questions:

Hint: The Bibliography at the back of this book lists several books and articles to help you begin your research.

☆ What products does the company make or what services does it provide?

☆ How did your subject develop an interest in this field?

☆ In what areas of the United States or the world does the company operate?

Hint: Use the Readers' Guide to Periodical Literature or InfoTrac to find articles in such magazines or newspapers as U.S. News & World Report and The Wall Street Journal.

☆ How are the products or services of this company different from others currently available?

☆ How do these products or services affect the environment?

Hint: Your local Chamber of Commerce might have information about a particular industry or company.

Next, go to the library to find the answers to your questions.

Hold a Business & Industry Fair to share your findings with your class or school. Present an information forum, discussing the advantages of various companies and their products.

Extending Your Studies

LANGUAGE ARTS **Your task:** *To conduct a debate.* Two of the subjects in this unit express opposing opinions: Antonia Hernández believes, "To be a really good lawyer, you have to be a well-rounded person," while, according to Oscar de la Renta, "To do something very well, you have to do only one thing."

Work with a group of four classmates, two to a team. Each team will debate one side of the issue. After you have chosen your position, organize your arguments. Work with your teammate to find examples in the biographies you have read to support this opinion.

State your argument in debate-style language. For example, if you were going to propose changing the school calendar, you might say "Resolved: That school should remain open four days of every week year-round." You will also have a chance to give a rebuttal, or answer, after you have heard what the other team says.

Stage your debate for your class or for another class. Listen carefully to the other team and take notes as the members speak, so that your rebuttal will be clear. Appoint one or more judges to choose the more convincing team.

You might also want to read about famous debates in history, such as the Lincoln-Douglas debates of 1862. Perhaps you can arrange to visit a debating club or team in your school or community.

MATH **Your task:** *To collect data that show the cost and effectiveness of three ways of advertising a product.* Imagine that you have manufactured a new product or invented a new service. You believe that it will benefit many people, so you decide to advertise.

How will you get your message to the public? Which method of communication will you choose—letter, telephone, or television? Do some research to discover the cost and the number of people reached by each of these three methods. You may need to find information in a library or contact some businesses in your community to estimate these numbers.

Draw on chart paper three large outlines of a mailbox, a telephone, and a television. Gather your data and display it clearly inside or near the appropriate picture. Include rate cards, price lists, and any other information you have found. Talk with your classmates about your data. Decide together which method of advertising provides the best buy for your product or service and which is the best way to reach the largest number of people who might buy your product.

SOCIAL STUDIES **Your task:** *To write a letter to a member of the United States Senate or House of Representatives.* In this unit you read that Ileana Ros-Lehtinen is a member of the United States House of Representatives. This is one half of Congress, which is the legislative, or lawmaking, branch of the federal government in Washington, D.C. The other half of Congress is the U.S. Senate.

Each state elects two senators, for a total of 100. The number of representatives from a state depends on that state's total population. Find out how many representatives are in the House and how many your state elects. Your library or a local newspaper should have the names and addresses of your senators and representatives.

Work with a partner to write a letter to your senator or representative. Give your opinion about an issue that is in the news. You might also wish to ask for information about some area of the federal government. Perhaps some day you will visit Washington, DC, to see your elected lawmakers during a working session of Congress!

WRITING WORKSHOP

In Units 2 and 3, you wrote biographical sketches of a friend and of a family or community member. The information for these sketches came from your memory or from interviews. For this sketch, you will use books, magazines, and other sources to write a **researched biography**.

PREWRITING

Select a subject: To begin your **prewriting** activities, write the names of three or four people whose work or life interests you. Next to each name write two phrases that describe this person. Then choose the person who most appeals to you.

Another approach would be to start with a particular field. Perhaps you want to find out more about being an astronaut, or you might be studying ballet or writing a play and would like to learn about someone who is a professional in one of those fields. You might go to the library and read newspaper or magazine articles about these topics. Then you might identify astronaut Ellen Ochoa, playwright Luis Valdes, or prima ballerina Evelyn Cisneros as good subjects for your biography. Look for subjects who are noteworthy and for whom there are source materials available.

Locate materials: Use the card catalog or database in your library to find books on your subject. Look up your subject's name and write down the title and call number of each book about your subject. Here are some examples:

Author	Title	Call Number
Dorros, Arthur	*Rainforest Secrets*	J574.52642 Dor
Gillies, John	*Señor Alcalde*	BIO CIS
Sinnott, Susan	*Extraordinary Hispanic Americans*	J920.00 Sin

A librarian can help you locate the materials you need and suggest other sources. The *Readers' Guide to Periodical Literature* lists magazine articles. Look at the Bibliography on pages 244–246 for additional resources.

Limit your topic: You may become so interested in your subject that you want to tell all about the person. Do not try to cover the person's entire life. Concentrate on one theme or one or two significant events. You'll draw a clearer picture of your subject if you tell one idea completely than if you try to cover too much ground.

Take notes: As you read, take notes on index cards. Write your notes in your own words. If you want to use a subject's exact words, copy the quote carefully and use quotation marks. On each index card, write the title and page number of the reference you have used. On a separate sheet, make a list of all your sources, listing author, publisher, and date and place of publication.

Organize your notes: Arrange your cards in categories, such as Early Family Life or Role Models. Narrow your topic and decide what is important to your essay and what you will leave out. Think about what you want your readers to learn about your subject.

Put your ideas in a logical order. Many biographies use chronological, or time, order, presenting life events as the subject grows up.

DRAFTING

When you are ready to write a **draft**, begin with an interesting fact or quotation to catch your reader's attention. Continue to write the ideas that come to mind. Do not worry about making it perfect. You will check for word usage and spelling later.

Include a bibliography: At the end of your biography, list the materials you have used in alphabetical order. Use this form for books:

Author	Title	City Published	Publisher	Copyright Date
Gillies, John.	Señor Alcalde: A Biography of Henry Cisneros.	Minneapolis:	Dillon Press,	1988.
Heller, Jeffrey.	Joan Baez: Singer with a Cause.	Chicago:	Children's Press,	1991.

Use this form for magazine articles:

Author	Article Title	Magazine Title	Date	Page Numbers
Hughes, Robert.	"Taking Back His Own Gods."	Time,	22 Feb. 1993,	p. 68.

REVISING

Put your biography aside for a few days. Then, with the help of another student who will act as your editor, evaluate and **revise** your work. See the directions for writers and student editors below.

Directions for Writers: Before you give your biography to your student editor, ask yourself these questions:

☆ Does my opening keep the reader's attention?

☆ Are the ideas in a logical order?

☆ Have I included quotes from the subject?

☆ Have I drawn a clear picture of my subject?

☆ Does the ending summarize the focus of my biography?

Make notes for your next draft or revise your work before you give it to your student editor. Then ask your editor to read your work. Listen carefully to his or her suggestions. If they seem helpful, use them to improve your writing when you revise your work.

Directions for Student Editors: Read the work carefully and respectfully, remembering that your purpose is to help the writer do his or her best work. Keep in mind that an editor should always make positive, helpful comments that point to specific parts of the writing. After you read the work, use these questions to help direct your comments:

☆ What do I like most about the biography?

☆ What would I like to know more about?

☆ Is the writing clear and logical?

☆ Has the writer used specific details to describe the subject?

☆ Do the subject's character and achievements come through?

PROOFREADING

When you are satisfied that your work says what you want it to say, **proofread** it for errors in spelling, punctuation, capitalization, and grammar. Then make a neat, final copy of your biography.

PUBLISHING

After you revise and proofread your biography, you are ready to **publish** it. Give a presentation to your class, sharing your writing and describing your research sources and methods. Answer any questions your classmates have or refer them to your bibliography for further reading.

Put your work together with the biographies of the students in your class and set up a reading file. Read some of the other biographies, then use the bibliographies to find more information about a person or topic that interests you.

GLOSSARY

PRONUNCIATION KEY

Vowel Sound	Symbol	Respelling
a as in *hat*	a	HAT
a as in *day, date, paid*	ay	DAY, DAYT, PAYD
vowels as in *far, on*	ah	FAHR, AHN
vowels as in *dare, air*	ai	DAIR, AIR
vowels as in *saw, call, pour*	aw	SAW, KAWL, PAWR
e as in *pet, debt*	eh	PEHT, DEHT
e as in *seat, chief*; **y** as in *beauty*	ee	SEET, CHEEF, BYOO-tee
e in a syllable that ends with a vowel *(Spanish)*	eh	MEH
e in a syllable that ends with a consonant *(Spanish)*	ee	koh-MEHR
vowels as in *learn, fur, sir*	er	LERN, FER, SER
i as in *sit, bitter*; **ee** as in *been*	ih	SIHT, BIHT-uhr, BIHN
i as in *mile*; **y** as in *defy*; **ei** as in *height*	eye	MEYEL, dee-FEYE, HEYET
i as in *Latina (Spanish)*	ee	lah-TEE-na
o as in *go*	oh	GOH
vowels as in *boil, toy*	oi	BOIL, TOI
vowels as in *foot, could*	o͝o	FO͝OT, KO͝OD
vowels as in *boot, rule, suit*	oo	BOOT, ROOL, SOOT
vowels as in *how, out, bough*	ow	HOW, OWT, BOW
vowels as in *up, come*	u	UP, KUM
vowels as in *use, use, few*	yoo	YOOZ, YOOS, FYOO
vowels as in *guapo (Spanish)*	wa	GWAH-poh
vowels as in *buena (Spanish)*	weh	BWEH-nah
vowels in unaccented syllables *(schwas) again, upon, sanity*	uh	uh-GEHN, uh-PAHN, SAN-uh-tee

Consonant Sound	Symbol	Respelling
ch as in *choose, reach*	ch	CHOOZ, REECH
g as in *go, dig*	g	GOH, DIHG
g before **e** or **i**, as in *gitana (Spanish)*	g	hee-TAH-nah
gh as in *rough, laugh*	f	RUF, LAF

h as in *who, whole*	h	HOO, HOHL
h as in *haga (Spanish)*	(silent)	AH-gah
j as in *jar*; **dg** as in *fudge*; **g** as in *gem*	j	JAHR, FUJ, JEHM
j as in *hota (Spanish)*	h	HOH-tah
k as in *king*; **c** as in *come*; **ch** as in *Christmas*	k	KIHNG, KUM, KRIHS-muhs
ll as in *llama (Spanish)*	y	YAH-mah
ñ as in *niña (Spanish)*	ny	NEE-nyeh
ph as in *telephone*	f	TEHL-uh-fohn
rr *(rolled)* as in *carreta (Spanish)*	rr	kah-RREH-tah
s as in *treasure*; **g** as in *bourgeois*	zh	TREH-zhuhr, boor-ZHWAH
s as in *this, sir*	s	THIS, SER
sh as in *ship*	sh	SHIHP
th as in *thin*	th	THIHN
th as in *this*	th	THIHS
wh as in *white*	wh	WHEYET
x as in *fix, axle*	ks	LIHKS, AK-suhl
x as in *exist*	gz	ihg-ZIHST
z as in *zero*; **s** as in *chasm*	z	ZEE-roh, KAZ-uhm

abstract (ab-STRAKT) *adj.* a type of art that does not attempt to picture something as it is in life, 64

accountant (uh-KOWN-tuhnt) *n.* someone who keeps track of the money spent and received by a person or business, 155

accused (uh-KYOOZD) *v.* charged with an offense, 121

acquired (ah-KWEYERD) *v.* gained as one's own, 18

advance (uhd-VANTS) *n.* money paid before work is done, 10

advocate (AD-vuh-kuht) *n.* a defender, 140

alienated (AY-lee-uh-nay-tuhd) *v.* to feel like one doesn't belong to a group, 184

ambitious (am-BIH-shuhs) *adj.* wanting to reach a goal; challenging, 174

analysis (uh-NA-luh-suhs) *n.* the study of a person's mind, 148

ancestors (AN-sehs-tuhrz) *n. pl.* people from whom a person is descended, 156

articulate (ahr-TIH-kyuh-luht) *adj.* able to speak clearly and effectively, 185

aspects (AS-pehkts) *n. pl.* features; the ways that something looks, 156

assigned (uh-SEYEND) *v.* appointed to a job, 121

audiotapes (AWD-ee-oh-tayps) *n. pl.* sound recordings, 149

banished (BA-nihsht) *v.* driven out, 200

bewilderment (bih-WIHL-duhr-muhnt) *n.* the feeling of being confused or puzzled, 175

bilingual (beye-LIHNG-wuhl) *adj.* using two languages, 219

biosphere (BEYE-uh-sfihr) *n.* all of the living things of the Earth together with their environment, 130

bizarre (buh-ZAHR) *adj.* odd; fantastic; crazy, 27

brash (BRASH) *adj.* reckless; impulsive, 92

brutality (broo-TA-luh-tee) *n.* cruelty, 220

carreta (kah-RREH-tah) *n.* Spanish for *cart*, 46

caucus (KAW-kuhs) *n.* people who meet because they have common interests, 185

chaos (KAY-ahs) *n.* a state of complete confusion, 119

charisma (kuh-RIHZ-muh) *n.* magnetic appeal; charm, 174

Chief Executive Officer the leader of an organization or business, 201

choreographing (KAWR-ee-uh-graf-ihng) *v.* designing dances, 94

circumstances (SUR-kuhm-stahns-uhz) *n. pl.* situation, 18

civil liberties (SIH-vuhl LIH-buhr-teez) freedom from unnecessary government restrictions, 182

civil rights the rights of personal liberty granted by the U.S. Constitution and acts of Congress, 221

cleaver (KLEE-vuhr) *n.* large knife used for cutting meat, 119

colleagues (KAHL-eegz) *n. pl.* people who do the same kind of work, 131

colon (KOH-luhn) *n.* the lower part of the large intestine, 137

compromise (KAHM-pruh-meyez) *v.* give away something to gain something in return, 87

concept (KAHN-sehpt) *n.* idea, 67

confirmation (kahn-fuhr-MAY-shuhn) *n.* proof; evidence, 86, 177

consumed (kuhn-SOOMD) *v.* fully occupied, 29

counteract (kown-tuh-RAKT) *v.* to cancel; offset, 138

credentials (krih-DEHN-shuhlz) *n. pl.* papers that show a person is qualified to do something, 122

deadlines (DEHD-leyenz) *n. pl.* dates by which something must be finished, 20

declaim (dih-KLAYM) *v.* to recite a poem or other work in a dramatic way, 47

decor (day-KOHR) *n.* decoration; the decorative scheme of a room, 86

defected (dih-FEHKT-uhd) *v.* abandoned one country to live in another, 94

deference (DEH-fuhr-ruhns) *n.* respect due an older or wiser person, 201

depict (dih-PIHKT) *v.* show; represent, 104

determination (dih-tehr-muh-NAY-shuhn) *n.* a firm intention; persistence, 83

devastated (DEH-vuh-stayt-uhd) *v.* destroyed; ruined, 103

distinct (dih-STIHNGKT) *adj.* different; separate, 18, 102

diversity (duh-VUHR-suh-tee) *n.* variety, 130

divisive (duh-VEYE-sihv) *adj.* creating a lack of unity; causing to split apart, 184

doctorate (DAHK-tuh-ruht) *n.* the rank or title of doctor, or Ph.D., earned after years of academic study and research after college, 130

document (DAH-kyoo-muhnt) *v.* to record; to find evidence of, 131

dynamic (deye-NA-mihk) *adj.* having a lot of energy, 46

economically (eh-kuh-NAH-mih-kuh-lee) *adv.* having to do with money, 219

emphasize (EHM-fuh-seyez) *v.* stress or feature, 102

emphasizing (EHM-fuh-seyez-ihng) *v.* stressing; putting importance on, 194

energizing (EH-nuhr-jeyez-ihng) *v.* giving out strength and eagerness, 102

enraged (ihn-RAYJD) *adj.* angered, 203

enriched (ihn-RIHCHT) *v.* made more valuable, 148

enterprising (EHN-tuhr-preye-zihng) *adj.* being spirited and independent, 101

environment (ihn-VEYE-ruhn-muhnt) *n.* the conditions that affect the way a plant, animal, or person develops, 218

exclusive (ihks-KLOO-sihv) *n.* a contract that limits someone to work only for one person or group, 85

exhilarating (ihg-ZIHL-uh-rayt-ihng) *adj.* exciting, 92

exiles (EHG-zeyelz) *n. pl.* people who are forced to leave their homeland; those who do not fit into a community or culture, 148

exquisite (ehk-SKWIH-zuht) *adj.* carefully done; precise, 147

extended family (ihk-STEHND-uhd FAM-uh-lee) a family that includes relatives such as grandparents, cousins, uncles, and aunts, 44

fanatic (fuh-NAT-ihk) *adj.* obsessed; too enthusiastic, 74
fate (FAYT) *n.* the belief that events will happen in a certain way, 46
fierce (FEERS) *adj.* wild; intense, 17
franchise (FRAN-cheyez) *n.* a right granted to sell something in a particular area, 194
frenetically (fruh-NEHT-ihk-lee) *adv.* frantically; energetically, 29

guardian (GAHR-dee-uhn) *n.* one who takes care of another person, 8
guerrilla (guh-RIH-luh) *n.* a soldier who doesn't belong to a regular army; guerrillas often fight their enemy with quick, surprise attacks, 132

heiress (AR-uhs) *n.* a woman whose family is wealthy, 212
hothouse (HAHT-hows) *adj.* grown in a greenhouse, 18
humiliated (hyoo-MIHL-ee-ayt-uhd) *v.* ashamed; embarrassed, 7

identity (eye-DEHN-tuh-tee) *n.* the collection of qualities that makes a person different from others, 219
impeccably (ihm-PEH-kuh-blee) *adv.* perfectly; without error, 209
incentives (ihn-SEHN-tihvz) *n. pl.* encouragements; motivations, 73
incorporated (ihn-KAWR-puh-ray-tuhd) *v.* blended or combined into, 65
instilled (ihn-STIHLD) *v.* put in little by little, 220
insulated (IHN-suh-layt-uhd) *v.* kept unaware; shielded, 94
internal (ihn-TUR-nuhl) *adj.* inside, 36
interracial (ihn-tuhr-RAY-shuhl) *adj.* involving or concerned with members of different heritages, 66
intrigued (ihn-TREEGD) *adj.* caused interest or curiosity, 100

introverted (IHN-truh-vurht-uhd) *adj.* someone whose attention is focused on himself or herself, not on the outside world, 36

jolt (JOHLT) *n.* a sudden feeling of shock, surprise, or disappointment, 36

Latina (lah-TEE-na) *adj.* a woman from a Spanish-speaking country or with a cultural background from a Spanish-speaking country. A *Latina* is female. *Latino* refers to males or a group of males and females, 17

lavishly (LA-vihsh-lee) *adv.* richly; expensively, 212

line *n.* collection of clothing designs, 210

literally (LIH-tuh-ruh-lee) *adv.* actually, 73

luxurious (luhg-ZHOOR-ee-uhs) *adj.* of the finest and richest kind; elegant, 211

luxury (LUK-shuh-ree) *n.* something adding to pleasure but not necessary, 27

machete (muh-SHEH-tee) *n.* a large, heavy knife, 44

makeup (MAY-kuhp) *n.* the way in which the parts of something are put together; its composition, 157

mandate (MAN-dayt) *n.* a command, 37

matriarchal (may-tree-AHR-kuhl) *adj.* a type of family that is headed by a woman, 63

mentor (MEHN-tawr) *n.* a trusted guide or teacher, 48

meteorite (MEE-tee-uh-reyet) *n.* a piece of matter from space that lands on Earth, 158

migrant workers (MEYE-gruhnt) people who move from place to place picking crops, 146

muse (MYOOZ) *n.* a source of inspiration, 45

mythic (MIHTH-ihk) *adj.* imaginary, 37

obsessed (uhb-SEHST) *v.* thought about constantly, 28

offbeat (awf-BEET) *adj.* unusual; odd, 158

one-dimensional (WUHN duh-MEHN-shuhn-uhl) *adj.* lacking depth; too simple, 85

paralysis (puh-RA-luh-suhs) *n.* the state of not being able to move, 72

partisan (PAHR-tuh-zuhn) *adj.* strongly supporting one side, party, or person, sometimes unreasonably, 185

pediatrician (pee-dee-uh-TRIH-shuhn) *n.* a doctor who treats children, 137

perception (puhr-SEHP-shuhn) *n.* belief; feeling, 104

persevere (puhr-suh-VIHR) *v.* to keep at something regardless of opposition or discouragement, 76

persisted (puhr-SIHST-uhd) *v.* continued; stayed with it, 93

persistence (puhr-SIHS-tuhnts) *n.* determination; continuing to work at something, 193

persistent (puhr-SIHS-tuhnt) *adj.* determined; insistent, 175

perspective (puhr-SPEHK-tihv) *n.* the ability to see the true importance of things, 211

phenomenal (fih-NAH-muh-nuhl) *adj.* remarkable; extraordinary, 100

phenomenon (fih-NAH-muh-nahn) *n.* an unusual fact or occurrence, 146

potential (puh-TEHN-shuhl) *n.* a possibility; something that can develop, 186

potential (puh-TEHN-shuhl) *adj.* possible, 193

precious (PREH-shuhs) *adj.* of great value, 147

prejudice (PREH-juh-duhs) *n.* suspicion or intolerance of other cultural, religious, or other groups, 35

premier (prih-MYEER) *adj.* most important; best, 92

prestige (preh-STEEZH) *n.* standing in the community, 209

prestigious (preh-STIH-juhs) *adj.* important; famous, 18

principal (PRIHN-suh-puhl) adj. leading, 94

prodigy (PRAHD-uh-jee) *n.* a highly talented child, 94

profound (pruh-FOWND) *adj.* deep; important, 9

proverbs (PRAHV-uhrbz) *n. pl.* brief sayings containing wisdom, 200

psychologist (seye-KAHL-uh-jihst) *n.* one who studies the mind and behavior, 146

pursue (puhr-SOO) *v.* to follow, 155

quest (KWEHST) *n.* a crusade; intention, 140

radical (RAD-uh-kuhl) *adj.* extreme, 36
recall (rih-KAWL) *v.* to remove an elected official by a vote of the people, 175
recruiter (rih-KROOT-uhr) *n.* someone who seeks new students, 19
refugee (reh-fyoo-GEE) *adj.* one who leaves one country to live in another country, 27
rejection (rih-JEHK-shuhn) *adj.* refusing; not accepting of something, 148
relevant (REH-luh-vuhnt) *adj.* appropriate; related to people's needs, 100
rickety (RIH-kuh-tee) *adj.* shaky; likely to fall or break, 121
rival (REYE-vuhl) *adj.* competitor, 203

sacrificing (SAK-ruh-feyes-ihng) *v.* giving up, 220
sanctuary (SANGK-chuh-wehr-ee) *n.* a place of protection; a haven, 10
scripts (SKRIHPTS) *n. pl.* written texts of plays, movies, or TV shows, 28
security (sih-KYOO-ruh-tee) *n.* safety; protection, 27
sentiment (SEHN-tuh-muhnt) *n.* a thought that is influenced by emotion, 48
sequel (SEE-kwuhl) *n.* a work that continues the story told in an earlier book, movie, or other story, 10
situation comedy (sih-chuh-WAY-shuhn KAH-muh-dee) a television comedy series that features the same characters each week, 28
sociology (soh-see-AH-luh-gee) *n.* the study of people and how they live together, 27
sorghum (SAWR-guhm) *n.* a plant used to make sugar syrup, 174
stable (STAY-buhl) *adj.* steady; secure, 47
staid (STAYD) *adj.* serious; proper, 182
stamina (STAM-uh-nuh) *adj.* having staying power; enduring, 93

sustaining (suh-STAYN-ihng) *v.* keeping something going; supporting, 104

techniques (tehk-NEEKS) *n. pl.* methods of bringing about a result, 157

tolerance (TAH-luh-ruhnts) *n.* patience; sympathy, 139

touchstone (TUCH-stohn) *n.* the standard by which others are judged, 10

transform (tranz-FAWRM) *v.* change, 103

transition (tran-ZIH-shuhn) *n.* a movement from one condition to another, 130

transmits (tranz-MIHTS) *v.* broadcasts, 121

triumph (TREYE-uhmf) *n.* great success, 121

ultimate (UL-tuh-muht) *adj.* highest; most extreme, 210

unconventional (uhn-kuhn-VEHN-shuhn-uhl) *adj.* out of the ordinary; not usual, 194

undercurrents (UHN-duhr-kuhr-uhnts) *n. pl.* hidden opinions or feelings, 28

unstable (uhn-STAY-buhl) *adj.* changing rapidly; uncertain, 156

valedictorian (va-luh-dihk-TOHR-ee-uhn) *n.* the student, usually with the highest grades, who gives the address at a graduation ceremony, 201

vicious (VIH-shuhs) *adj.* cruel; mean, 184

vignettes (vihn-YEHTS) *n. pl.* brief stories or descriptions, 9

BIBLIOGRAPHY

Alvarado, Linda

"Linda Alvarado." *Notable Hispanic American Women.* Detroit: Gale Research, 1993, p. 11.

"Lady in the Hard Hat." *Minority Business Entrepreneur,* July/August 1989, pp. 6–9.

Alvarez, Julia

Alvarez, Julia. *How the Garcia Girls Lost Their Accents.* Chapel Hill: Algonquin Books, 1991.

Garner, Dwight. "A Writer Shares Her View of Two Different Worlds." *Middlebury Magazine,* Summer 1991, pp. 25–27.

Baca, Judith

Martinez, Yleana. "Judith F. Baca." *Notable Hispanic American Women.* Detroit: Gale Research, 1993, pp. 35–38.

Neumaier, Diane. "Judy Baca: Our People Are the Internal Exiles." *Making Face, Making Soul,* ed. by Gloria Anzaldúa. San Francisco: Aunt Lute Foundation Books, 1990.

Bujones, Fernando

Fanger, Iris. "On the Road to Boston." *Dance Magazine,* May 1, 1991, pp. 48–52.

Gruen, John. "Spotlight on: Fernando Bujones." *Dance Magazine,* Oct. 1976, pp. 63–67.

Cisneros, Sandra

Cisneros, Sandra. *The House on Mango Street.* New York: Vintage Books, 1991.

Tabor, Mary B.W. "A Solo Traveler in Two Worlds." *New York Times,* Jan. 7, 1993, p. C1.

Colón, Miriam

Shepard, Richard F. "For Street Troupe, at 20, Life's Both Buena y Good." *New York Times,* April 18, 1987.

Hurley, Joseph. "A Bilingual Success Story with Spanish Roots." *New York Newsday,* April 14, 1987.

Dallmeier, Francisco
Dallmeier, Francisco. "Conserving Biodiversity: Director's Report." *Biodiversity News* (Smithsonian MAB Program), Winter/Spring, 1994.

de la Renta, Oscar
Duffy, Martha. "Mais Oui, Oscar." *Time*, Feb. 8, 1993, p. 68.

Howell, Georgina. "Charmed Circles." *Vogue*, Sept. 1989, p. 730.

Escalante, Jaime
Mathews, Jay. *Escalante: The Best Teacher in America.* New York: Henry Holt, 1988.

Estefan, Gloria
Estefan, Gloria, with Kathryna Casey. "My Miracle." *Ladies Home Journal,* August, 1990.

Stefoff, Rebecca. *Gloria Estefan.* New York: Chelsea House Publishers, 1991.

Estés, Clarissa Pinkola
Estés, Clarissa Pinkola. *Women Who Run with the Wolves.* New York: Ballantine Books, 1992.

King, Patricia. "The Call of the Wild Woman." *Newsweek,* Dec. 21, 1992, p. 59.

Goizueta, Roberto
Huey, John. "The World's Best Brand." *Fortune,* May 31, 1993, p. 44.

Pendergrast, Mark. *For God, Country, and Coca-Cola.* New York: Charles Scribner's Sons, 1993.

Hernández, Antonia
Higuera, Jonathan J. "Antonia Hernández." *Notable Hispanic American Women.* Detroit: Gale Research, 1993.

Gross, Liza. "Antonia Hernández: MALDEF's Legal Eagle," *Hispanic* Magazine, Dec. 1990, pp. 17–18.

Laviera, Tato
Laviera, Tato. *AmeRícan.* Houston: Arte Público Press, 1985.

Laviera, Tato. *Mainstream Ethics.* Houston: Arte Público Press, 1988.

Mohr, Nicholasa

Mohr, Nicholasa. *Felita.* New York: Dial, 1977.

Garcia-Johnson, Ronie-Richele. "Nicholasa Mohr." *Notable Hispanic American Women.* Detroit: Gale Research, 1993.

Novello, Antonia

Krucoff, Carol. "Antonia Novello: A Dream Come True." *The Saturday Evening Post,* May/June 1991, p. 38.

"Novello, Antonia." *Current Biography Yearbook,* 1992. New York: H.W. Wilson, 1992.

Ocampo, Adriana

Telgen, Diane, and Jim Kamp, eds. "Adriana C. Ocampo." *Notable Hispanic American Women.* Detroit: Gale Research, 1993, p. 295.

Olmos, Edward James

Meyers, Laura. "One Year Later—A Talk with Edward James Olmos." *Los Angeles Magazine,* April, 1993.

"Olmos, Edward James." *Current Biography*, July, 1992, pp 36-39.

Peña, Federico

Arias, Anna Maria. "Federico Peña: Quick Study." *Hispanic Magazine,* June 1993, pp. 16-21.

"Peña, Federico." *Current Biography*, October, 1993, pp 36-39.

Ros-Lehtinen, Ileana

Balmaseda, Liz. "Ileana Ros-Lehtinen Charges the Hill." *The Miami Herald,* Nov. 19, 1989, p. 1G.

Gonsior, Marian. "Ileana Ros-Lehtinen." *Notable Hispanic American Women.* Detroit: Gale Research, 1993.

Santeiro, Luis

Collins, Marion. "Que Pasa, Luis?" New York *Daily News,* June 21, 1987.

Dolen, Christine. "Lady from Havana in Town." *The Miami Herald,* Nov. 10, 1991, p. 1l.

Unit 1: Literature

These magazines present students' and adult writers' work, as well as articles that discuss the craft of writing.

The Horn Book (includes book reviews for young people)
Stone Soup (a literary magazine for young people)
Story (a literary magazine for advanced readers)
Writer's Digest (features articles about ways to improve writing and interviews with writers

Look for these books to read more about Cuban American emigration:

Gernand, Renee. *The Peoples of North America: The Cuban-Americans.* New York: Chelsea House, 1988.

Grenquist, Barbara. *Recent American Immigrants: Cubans.* New York: Franklin Watts, 1991.

Unit 2: Fine Arts and Performance

The following magazines explore the concerns and happenings of the art world.

American Art (profiles American artists)
American Artist (discusses artistic techniques and materials)

These materials provide information about specific performing arts.

Backstage (newspaper highlighting the activities of actors, singers, and dancers)
Callback (magazine focusing on the business aspects of show business)

Dance Magazine (interviews with dancers, news of national dance companies)

Dance America (newsletter of dance activities in communities across the U.S.)

You can find another biography of Edward James Olmos—in addition to reading about thirteen other prominent Mexican American men and women—in this book:

Morey, Janet, and Wendy Dunn. *Famous Mexican Americans*. New York: Cobblehill Books/Dutton, 1989.

Read more about Miriam Colón and other noted Puerto Ricans in this book:

Newlon, Clarke. *Famous Puerto Ricans*. New York: Dodd, Mead, 1975.

A historical view of art and architecture is given in this book:

Glubok, Shirley. *The Art of the Spanish in the United States and Puerto Rico*. New York: Macmillan, 1972.

Meet Cuban American ballet dancer Evelyn Cisneros by reading this book:

Simon, Charnan. *Evelyn Cisneros, Prima Ballerina*. Chicago: Childrens Press, 1990.

Unit 3: The Sciences and Mathematics

To learn more about science and health, watch for "Nova" specials on public television. These programs discuss scientific breakthroughs and interview noted scientists. You might also enjoy the following magazines:

American Health (presents news in medicine and health)

Byte (for and about computer programmers)
Discover (news of science)
The Futurist (theories of the future)
Popular Science (the mechanics of scientific instruments)

To learn more about such scientists as Adriana Ocampo and Antonia Novello, look for this book in your library:

Noble, Iris. *Contemporary Women Scientists of America*. New York: Julian Messner, 1979.

Learn more about Jaime Escalante with this book or video:

Stand and Deliver. Warner Bros.: 1988
Edwards, Nicholas. *Stand and Deliver*. New York: Scholastic, 1989.

Unit 4: Public Service and Business

For up-to-date news on government, politics, and economics around the world, look for the magazines *Newsweek*, *Time*, and *U.S. News and World Report*.

You might also like to read about Texas Railroad Commissioner Lena Guerrero, another Mexican American in public service, in this book of biographies:

Sinnott, Susan. *Extraordinary Hispanic Americans*. Chicago: Childrens Press, 1991.

INDEX